THE WATCHER'S WEB

Tennille Jo Mortensen

Published by Tennille Mortensen

ISBN 978-1-7370726-0-7

DEDICATION

For anyone who has ever felt alone in this crazy world and
to my ever-supportive family members who have been
my greatest cheerleaders

CONTENTS

Prelude

"Master Burdock?" The elder man cocked his head to the side at the approach of his young apprentice.

"Yes, Watcher Minnion, what is it?" he asked, though he had already felt the vibrations of the web himself. His bald head reflected the moonlight, and he stroked his white goatee as he awaited the young man's response.

"I have found a young man at the point of extinction," he reported.

"And?" his master prodded, speaking so softly his voice harmonized perfectly with the cool night breeze.

"He still has attachments, Master, though he pushes them away, the strands are bound securely. I fear he will extinguish himself if we do not intervene," Watcher Minnion explained.

"So, you recommend?" Master Burdock stared intently with his gray eyes.

"We can bring him here, sir. He can live among us," Watcher Minnion was pleading now.

"The rules of the web are enforced for a reason, young Minnion. What if his attachments seek him out? What will happen at his discovery – the heartache, the pain? What becomes of the web then?" the sage probed further.

"But Master Burdock, if we do nothing, he will be extinct. Then, what of the web? Is not the result the same in the eyes of his attachments? What of our vow of protection? Respectfully, sir, there must also be exceptions to every rule. Is he too not worth saving? Every strand is important, wise Master. Though he has temporarily blinded himself by his own emotions, I believe I can reach him. May I at least offer the alternative, sir?" Watcher Minnion petitioned, never breaking eye contact with his elder.

Master Burdock smiled at the young watcher. Though Minnion was unaware, Master Burdock's view of the web extended far beyond his own into the future. As a Master, he saw what Minnion could not concerning this strand, and it was certainly a much more complicated venture than Minnion could ever imagine. Yet, if successful, it would prove to save many others the watchers may not be able to reach. The proposition was risky, however. Allowing a strand with attachments to alter into the watcher's realm was rarely done. Often, those strands were already too set on their course to change the outcome, and there were complications with the altering process in those instances, so the watchers seldom intervened. The implications of failure could be far reaching, and yet Master Burdock was intrigued by this strand, intrigued by the possibilities, intrigued by the complexity.

"Well spoken, young Minnion. You will make a fine Master in time. Let this boy be the exception, if he will accept your offer, but bring him to me straight away. The web may well benefit from him, but he is the exception to the rule, and precautions must be taken. Now go before the time is spent." He sent Watcher Minnion away and summoned Valeressa to him.

"Yes, Master Burdock. You sent for me?" Valeressa appeared before him, her long red hair flowing behind her as she rushed forward.

"Ah, Valeressa. I have a job for you – a highly classified job that only you can do," he declared with a smile.

"Yes, master," her curiosity was piqued.

"Watcher Minnion is helping a young man to alter into our realm tonight, but this young man has secured attachments in his realm. Because of this, he cannot alter completely – his body will be left behind. This provision, as you may be aware, was made in order to protect our realm and the web, but I fear in this case, it could be an imminent danger to us all, particularly to the young man who comes tonight and the strands he can potentially save in the future. He is of more value to us in his own realm, but he must come to understand our realm first. He must feel of the peace here. Valeressa, your job

is to extract the body. You are the one among us who has retained the ability to touch in his realm and coexist in both realms without being seen. Another exception to the rule that continues to intrigue and baffle me. Once the body is extracted, you must put it in stasis – care for it – protect it," Master Burdock expounded.

"But sir, nothing like this has been done before. Extraction may only lead to extinction in the end anyway. The altering cannot be reversed, and I fear if he is somehow pulled back through the vortex, surely he will not survive to join with the body again," she argued, apprehension running down her spine like the blade of a knife.

"The choice has been made, Valeressa. It is a risk I am willing to take for the good of the web," he rebuked gently, the air of superiority lingering in the night after his voice had faded away.

"But Burdock," she persisted, dropping all pretenses of authority that separated the two, "you would risk a strand for this experiment of yours, or worse, a ripple in the web? You've always been the wisest of the masters, true and faithful to the vow."

"The strand would be extinct right now if we had not intervened, and this strand will not fare well in our realm. I have seen it, and yet there is one strong enough to save him if he will allow himself to be saved, Valeressa. We have always honored the choice of the strand, and I will continue to do so. I have seen three possibilities for this strand.

"Option one: He will remain with us, though he will never be one with us. He will never feel the real power of the brotherhood and sisterhood of the watchers or of the web because he is not truly one of us. He will still be attached to the web, whereas we have been severed from the web. For this reason, he will never see it as clearly as we do.

"Option two: He could choose extinction, or rather he will be extinguished by his own inability to choose a realm when the time comes for him to make the choice. The vortex will swallow him.

"Option three: He will successfully navigate back through the vortex and rejoin his realm with the body you have now been given charge to preserve and protect. If this happens the web will flourish with attachments. We as watchers cannot reattach strands; we can

only try to save the unattached from extinction. But this young man – this young man, Valeressa – he can maintain the integrity of the web in a capacity in which we never dreamed possible. I suspect that while he will not remember his time in our realm, he will retain the feelings of peace that he has felt here, and that will be enough to change the tide of his life. Certainly, there will be a ripple in the web as you have perceived, but not all ripples are bad, my dear child." His eyes were flashing with brightness and passion at the prospective of the third option.

"I will do as you bid, Master Burdock. I only hope this ends as you have seen in your third option – for the sake of the strand and the web," she said with reluctant obedience. Master Burdock was a valiant protector of the web, so she would have to trust his judgment in this matter. He could, after all, see the web on all levels and in all dimensions, and she could not.

"See to it, but a word of caution to you. Speak of this to no one for it would compromise everything, leading only to his extinction," he admonished, his gray eyes darkening with solemnity.

"Yes, Master Burdock," Valeressa turned to leave him, but paused to ask, "Master, who will save him?"

"One of his own kind – from his realm," he answered thoughtfully.

"But how?" she queried, searching for understanding to assuage the doubts that were threatening to sabotage her resolve.

"She will find a way. I have not seen a strand as strong as hers in these many years, which is why I'm putting his life and the web's sanctity in her hands. She is an unlikely heroine, indeed, who would have the potential to be a great master herself if she was to enter our realm," he spoke of this strand with great reverence and admiration as he often spoke of Valeressa herself.

Valeressa nodded and readied herself for the extraction. The words Burdock spoke were circling in her head like a vulture circling its prey – ready to attack her fears if only she would believe. She heard his words, "I have not seen a strand as strong as hers in these many years," echoing in her ears as she entered the vortex to cross realms. Master Burdock had never been wrong before, and she hoped this would not prove to be a first.

Chapter 1: Alone

ALONE

ALONE. Lost in a world of
Virtual reality.
ALONE. Subject to the confusion
Of invalid perception.
ALONE. Haunted by chaotic
Fears and failures.
ALONE. Not a place to call
Home.
ALONE. No one to share the
Feelings of the heart.
ALONE. No sense of the
Right direction.
ALONE. Engulfed in the tears
Of bewilderment.
ALONE. I am just me -
ALONE.

~ Jessie Watson

No one really knew Jessie Watson. From the front porch of her newest foster home, Jessie's hazel eyes fell upon rows and rows of houses, nearly identical in architecture, as though they had all been cut with the same cookie cutter. She came and went in the daily monotony of routine with neither a grand welcome at her first arrival nor a sorrowful farewell at her subsequent departure. Rarely were sentiments of friendship extended beyond a quaint greeting as the people around her continued in their habitual living, self-absorbed and oblivious to the web that bound everyone together in the great thread of humanity.

Jessie had been moving from one foster home to another as long as she could remember. As a high school senior, she found herself trying to settle into what would be her final foster home with an older couple named Hank and Margaret Moore. Although Margaret Moore told Jessie that she could call them by their first names, Jessie preferred to address them as Mr. and Mrs. Moore. She used that as a subconscious coping mechanism to protect herself from developing attachments to people she would have to leave behind.

Having grown accustomed to being overlooked throughout the years, Jessie had learned to keep to herself, so she spent most of her free time in her bedroom, alone. That's where she had first seen Shane Gunderson, who occupied the bedroom opposite hers in the house next door.

Shane, who happened to be incredibly good looking in Jessie's opinion, was in several of her classes at school, although he had no idea she existed. He rarely closed his blinds, which made it easy for Jessie to stare into his room without being seen from her vantage point. She found him to be an interesting subject to observe as he played video games with his buddies or worked on his homework until the early morning hours when he had been out too long with his friends after school. Although completely by accident, she had even caught a glimpse of him kissing his girlfriend, Nikki, though she quickly closed her blinds on that scene.

Jessie stared at him as she pulled her long, dark blonde hair into a ponytail. Shane was getting ready to go out for the evening, probably to the rivalry basketball game everyone had been chattering about for the past week at school. *Snap out of it*, her own thoughts interrupted her fresh daydream. Shane didn't know she existed, and she wasn't some kind of peeping tom. She always happened to be in her room, and he always happened to leave his blinds open, obviously unaware that he had a silent stalker mere yards away. She chuckled at the thought of herself as a stalker.

Her eyes drifted back to her calculus book, which was opened before her. She needed to finish her homework, but the tears came freely and familiarly to her eyes. Alone. The word resonated in her head. She once remembered someone reading a book to her when she was very young – a story about a little dalmatian puppy who no one noticed until he saved the day by spotting a fire. She could still see the black and white illustrations in her head. What strange memories a little girl holds onto! She felt as if the book was trying to prepare her to go unnoticed throughout her life. The puppy caused so much havoc trying to get noticed, but she wasn't about to bark on top of a fire hydrant for attention, and it was highly unlikely that she would ever do anything heroic. If someone was to notice her, all he or she would see is a plain girl in plain clothes doing plain things. She had once read a quote that seemed to sum her up: "I'm just a Raggedy Ann in a Barbie doll world."

Jessie knew that she didn't fit in anywhere– she was an extra puzzle piece without a place. She was a ward of the state until she graduated from high school, at which point she would be pushed out into the cold dark world to fend for herself. She sighed. She still had a few more months before she had to sort through all of that, although she was grateful that she had found a summer job the previous year to start saving for her uncertain future.

For now, Jessie struggled to get through each day. She always tried to arrive at school just in time to slide into her seat before the tardy bell rang. She spent nearly her entire lunch hour hiding out in the first stall of the bathroom or tucked away in an obscure corner of the girls' locker room. She tried not to let her mind linger on the posters in the hall announcing the upcoming dances, but she wasn't ignorant of the buzz of excitement as everybody made plans and speculated about who would ask whom. She had nothing to anticipate except another evening shut up in her bedroom, occasionally sneaking a peak at Shane when it was time for him to get ready for an upcoming event. She watched enviously as he picked out the perfect clothes and spent a little extra time on his naturally wavy brown hair. If she had to live a life of isolation, couldn't she be completely isolated from all of this?

Sometimes she drowned her loneliness in reading Jane Austen novels, which she borrowed from the library. Unfortunately, the feelings of hope and elation stirred by those novels always retreated as quickly as they came, leaving her once again in her dark and lonely cave of seclusion, void of even parental love and attention, let alone romance. She tried to think back over her life for memories of happiness, but it was like scaling a rock wall without a safety harness. Coming up short, she was left to gather the forlorn pieces of her shattered existence by herself, quietly tucking them back into the dark recesses of her subconscious where they could not bring her fresh pain.

Jessie's childhood and adolescence had been far from normal. She'd never learned to drive a car or gone to the movies with friends. She lived in fear of the uncertainty that buffeted her from place to place. She once caught a tiny glimmer of hope when she was selected as the Heart-to-Heart child on the local news, which allowed her to be spotlighted in hopes that someone would come forward to adopt her. That glimmer was quickly extinguished by reality when no inquiries were made on her behalf. Of course, she had been sixteen, a raisin among grapes in comparison to younger children in the foster care system. No one wanted her, and she had resigned herself to the plight of the lonely, although she never could quite reconcile herself to that fate. With that fleeting thought, she aimlessly closed her book and turned out the light.

Chapter 2: But Then

But Then

You think you're standing on a rock,
    But then it turns to sand.
You think the world is turning round,
    But then it's bouncing up and down.
You think the ice is frozen solid,
    But then it becomes a river wild.
You think you can depend on something,
    But then it fades into nothing.
You think your life is in control,
    But then it shrivels to chaos.
You think too often; you think too much,
    But then you find you're not actually thinking
    at all!

~ Jessie Watson

The next day after school, Jessie walked to the Moore's on her usual route. She looked up absently from the sidewalk in response to the strange feeling that someone was watching her. That's when she saw him: a boy about her age with short, sandy blonde hair and bright blue eyes. He was leaning against a tree with his arms folded, a boyish grin spread across his face. He winked at her. Looking away in disbelief, Jessie kept walking. Of course, she couldn't help but glance in his direction one more time to see if she had been daydreaming. He was still standing there in the exact same position, smiling at her.

She quickened her pace and found herself out of breath when she finally got to the house. Her heart was pounding, but she wasn't sure why. No one had ever looked at her the way that boy had. The instant their eyes had met, his image seemed permanently etched in her mind. She didn't bother looking for Shane that evening because she was too busy thinking of the boy at the tree.

Over the next week, Jessie found herself scanning crowds for the mysterious boy's face. Oddly enough, she always found those same piercing eyes staring back at her. She noticed him everywhere now – in her classes, at lunch, in the crowd of students leaving the high school, and always by the tree. How could she have not noticed him before? Why couldn't she put a name with his face? Maybe he was a delusion. Maybe after so much time by herself with no social contact, she had finally cracked up.

The next day followed the same pattern. Jessie caught several glimpses of the mysterious boy throughout the day. Every time she saw him, he was always staring back at her, and she turned away in embarrassment having been caught looking at him. She had come to expect to find him, and her embarrassment eventually gave way to self-consciousness because he never shifted his eyes in the slightest. She certainly didn't feel as though her appearance was enough to warrant attention from the homeliest boy, let alone this boy. Maybe she was getting ahead of herself. He probably wasn't staring at her in adoration, but it certainly wasn't repulsion either. She walked along her usual route after school, her eyes glued to the ground. When she neared the tree, however, she simply couldn't resist the urge to look up. Of course, he was there, anxiously eyeing her. She tried to look away, but couldn't seem to break his stare. Her pace slowed.

As she got closer, he motioned for her to come over. Since a very busy road bordered the sidewalk, she didn't see too much harm in stopping near the tree where he stood. He spoke first as she eyed him cautiously, yet with burning curiosity.

"You can see me now, can't you?" he asked, his voice animated.

"Of course, I can see you," she retorted, wondering if perhaps he was a figment of her overly active imagination. "Everyone can see you."

"You're further from the truth than you may know," came his whispered response.

Okay, she thought as she took a tiny step away from him, *now he's giving me the creeps.* Apparently, he took that as a sign of encouragement, and continued on, "I'm afraid you won't believe what I'm about to explain to you, but I am bound by a sacred vow to tell you. You see, I've been watching you for quite some time now."

"I've noticed," she gawked at him in alarm thinking back to the other night when she had referred to herself as a stalker. Perhaps this was her punishment. She felt as though she should have the urge to run away from him at this point, but her curiosity was stronger than her fear. Why had he suddenly appeared at school in just the right places, always staring at her? She inched a little farther away from him.

"I'm not here to hurt you, so please don't be afraid. Just hear me out," he pleaded. When she made no attempt to move again, he proceeded to talk.

"There is a place for people like us who have been left alone in the world. It's an unseen world for the most part, and I'm what we call a watcher." Jessie looked at him skeptically, but just as she was about to tell him she really had to be going, a group of teenagers approached on the sidewalk.

One of them called out to her as he drew near, "Hey, if you're just gonna stand there and stare at the tree, get outta the way." She immediately scooted off the sidewalk toward the strange boy, amazed that the group of passing kids didn't seem to notice him. Instead, they stared at her as if she was some kind of freak. The boy seemed unphased and picked up where he left off.

"I've been trying to tell you that they can't see me," but before he could finish, she interrupted him with the question, "Then, why can I see you?"

"You're one of us," he calmly answered. "Well, you will be one of us soon." She glanced at him skeptically as she started to walk away, but he jumped out in front of her. "Please, hear me out, okay?"

She nodded her head and muttered, "Can we at least go behind the tree so people aren't staring at me, thinking I'm talking to myself?" She walked to the back of the tree and sat down with her "ghost" following close behind.

"I'm Kaleb…Kaleb Scott," he casually introduced himself. "I think it might help if I start with my story first. My life turned upside down when my parents were killed in a car accident just after my high school graduation. I was so frustrated that the world kept going as if nothing had happened. After the funeral, my friends still went off to work their summer jobs, and the nightly anchormen moved on to another story. I think you felt the same way after you were featured on the news for the Heart-to-Heart adoption spotlight. Your hope was trampled when the world moved on without regard to your plight."

"How did you know about that? That happened over two years ago," she interrupted again. He chose to ignore her questions and continued his own story.

"My pain didn't go away, and I started to withdraw from my friends. I had never dealt with death before. My grandparents died when I was too young to remember them, so all my life was centered on my parents. When they were gone, I had nothing to live for anymore. I had no one. When I withdrew in my grief, my friends quit trying to come over, and they quit trying to call me. I decided one night that I couldn't go through life this way.

"My parents owned some property outside of town, where I would go to think. I hadn't talked to anyone in weeks. I was contemplating how fast everything in my life had changed as I sorted through my options. I had pretty much decided that I had nothing left to live for – that I couldn't force myself to live in that existence anymore. That's when I noticed a young man standing off to the side of a bunch of trees. He approached me cautiously and explained to me that he was a watcher. He told me I could enter his realm through a process called altering, and I would be able to see the world in a different light – that I would be able to help people who were lost like I was. The moment I decided to accept his offer, I altered into what I am today. One day I was there, and the next day no one could see me. No one noticed I was gone. No one blinked an eye. There was no news story on my disappearance, no posters, no missing person reports, nothing.

"You may wonder why we disappear, and it's hard to explain. You see, the world is like a giant spider web, where each person is a strand. The strands are all intricately connected, person to person. Most people prefer to live their lives oblivious to the fact that we are all connected, but as a watcher, I can see this web - the web of life, you could say. I feel the strands all woven together so tightly. I feel the vibrations as people or strands interact to form the bonds that hold the web together. It's as if I am a spider, watching for broken strands. I'm watching for that moment when a strand breaks free from the web and isn't immediately joined by another strand to reconnect it to the web. When that happens, I can offer that person the alternative of altering rather than ending his or her life or making other devastating choices like joining a bad crowd to find acceptance or drowning the pain with drugs and alcohol. Unfortunately, once someone chooses drugs, altering is no longer an option. They can't enter our realm with that kind of dependency. I watch for broken strands and try to help them alter into the watcher's realm, where they can have a home with others who have faced the same challenges in mortality."

She looked at him quizzically, as if she had been cast in the newest episode of the *Twilight Zone,* but she decided to play along. "So, why do the strands break?" she asked.

"You already know the answer, Jessie," Kaleb said as he ignored the small gasp she made when he said her name. "I told you that I've been watching you for a while now. Your strand has been broken for quite some time, but you could never see me. I think you have finally acknowledged how alone you really are. Only the lonely alter – those who have truly been forgotten and left completely on their own."

"I'm sorry. I don't know what to think. This is a little too comic book for me. I've got to be going," she stood up as she spoke, intent on running the rest of the way to the house.

"Wait! Please give me one more minute," he begged her. "You keep a collection of poetry you have written over the years hidden under your mattress, so no one can find it."

"How did you know that?" she whispered in shock. No living soul knew about her poetry. She had never shared it with anyone.

"That's why they call me a watcher," he replied. While his story had seemed so far-fetched at first, she somehow knew deep down that he was telling her the truth. She just didn't want to accept it.

"So, your mission is to rescue broken strands like me?"

"Pretty much. Once you age out of the foster care system, you're on your own. Many of the teens who are emancipated from foster care, simply end up living on the streets because they can't get the help they need. They have no money, no vehicle to get them to work, and no way to get an apartment without a security deposit or a parent to co-sign on the lease. I don't want that to happen to you. You don't have the life-line of friends that others do that will keep you bonded to the web." His eyes were full of concern as he spoke, and she knew in her heart that it was true. She had pushed these fears aside, hoping to find some sort of resolution to them, but she truly had no one to turn to. She was alone. Her eyes filled with tears.

"Why do you care so much about me anyway?" she demanded, suddenly feeling defensive.

He looked away as he carefully responded, "Like I said, I've been watching you for a while. Your strand hasn't been connected to anything. I'm surprised it's been so long, and you haven't altered yet. I've never quite seen a strand like yours. By the time people reach your age with your background, they usually give up, but you seem to bury your hurt, and keep going. I'm not sure if it's your hope that keeps you here or your stubbornness.

"I saw you the night of prom, when you walked to the park, crying silently by yourself with no one to comfort you. I think you started to give up a little on the hope. I was sure you'd alter after the Heart-to-Heart spotlight. If I could cry, I would have cried right along with you. I saw how the other strands vibrated toward yours, but each one thought someone else would be better suited. They excused themselves away from your strand. I saw your heart break over the weeks that followed. I saw you withdraw just like I did." He spoke softly to her, and he looked as if he wanted to give her a hug, but he hesitated and drew back.

"So, what now? What's going to happen to me?" she peppered him with questions.

"Now, we wait. You'll alter when the web senses that you're ready. None of us knows exactly how it happens. It's almost as if the web breaks you free from the loneliness. Once you alter, you can feel the love and hope that emanates from the web. You can feel the happiness of their connections with one another. I suppose we are the monitors that maintain the web in a sense, since we try to care for the strands that are forgotten. You realize when you alter that people don't forget on purpose. People like us kind of fall through the cracks, but it's going to be okay, Jessie." He smiled slightly at her again.

"I could still form bonds or whatever you call them, right?" she queried, not ready to give up on her life just yet.

"I guess so, but it's not probable," he responded matter-of-factly.

"Oh," she muttered under her breath as she stood up and started walking toward her house. She looked over her shoulder where she had left Kaleb sitting, but he wasn't following her this time. Jessie slowed her pace, mulling over their conversation in her mind, trying to make sense of it all.

The next morning on her way to school, she saw Kaleb leaning against the same tree with the same boyish grin on his face. *I guess it wasn't a dream or a nightmare after all,* she thought to herself, still skeptical. On the way home from school, she wasn't surprised to find him waiting for her again by the tree. She decided to move their little conference to a park near her house, where she often went to get away from the limited view her four bedroom walls offered. The playground equipment was dilapidated in comparison to the parks in the newer developments, so she was rarely interrupted. In fact, she had come to think of this place as her own personal sanctuary, where she often appeared to be a permanent fixture, the statue of a girl forgotten.

"So," Jessie murmured uncomfortably, "what are we supposed to do now?"

"I'm not sure, now that you mention it. I'm just waiting on you," Kaleb replied pleasantly. He certainly seemed to be enjoying himself.

"Okay…well if you don't mind, I have some homework to finish," she told him as she sat down on a warped picnic table and opened her backpack.

"What are you working on today?" he asked nonchalantly, as though coming here with her was a regular occurrence.

"Calculus," she groaned as she rolled her eyes and added, "I don't get it. I've never had a problem with math before, but this stuff must have been used to pave the road to the underworld." He laughed heartily in response.

"What exactly are you trying to figure out?" he seemed genuinely concerned. Why would he care about calculus homework? Didn't "a watcher" have more important things to worry about? Maybe he was trying to make her last days as a high school student less frustrating.

"Shouldn't you be more worried about chemistry?" she asked.

"Why would I care about chemistry?" he inquired with quirked eyebrows.

"Chemistry is all about bonds, and your specialty is broken bonds, isn't it?" she chuckled at her own corny joke, but so did he. She lightened up a little. Maybe this wouldn't be so bad after all. At least she had someone to talk to, someone who had no choice but to listen. She realized that she was completely at ease around Kaleb. She could be herself without feeling self-conscious. She had never felt that freedom before – freedom from her own self-judgments.

"Seriously, we are learning about derivatives, but the teacher doesn't really know how to explain the concept very well. When anyone asks him a question, he has to consult his answer book. He doesn't know anything about it himself," she explained, frustrated.

"Well, I'll see what I can do to help you out," Kaleb hovered over her shoulder looking at the calculus section to which she had turned.

"Are you allowed to do that?" she asked in awe.

"Why not? I'm just explaining a little calculus homework to you. It's not like I'm sending you answers to a test via ESP or anything," he answered.

"I'll take all the help I can get," she responded with a smile. He shook his head at her. He proved to be a very good personal tutor. By the time he was done explaining the concepts to her, she was able to breeze through her homework in no time. Unfortunately, the sun was already dipping behind the horizon.

"Well, I better get back before it gets too dark. Thanks for your help, Kaleb. I really appreciate you taking the time out of whatever it is you're really supposed to be doing to help me," she said.

"No problem. I'll see you tomorrow," he acknowledged as she walked away. She waved over her shoulder, feeling an accompanying wave of gratitude sweep over her. She slept restfully that night, knowing that there was someone out there waiting to see her tomorrow. The echo of his words hugged her goodnight as she drifted to sleep.

Interlude 1

Transporting the boy's body into stasis without injury had been no easy chore. He was much taller than she was with the muscular build of an adolescent male on the brink of adulthood. Valeressa mustered all her strength to drag him through the vortex until she could reach the point of stasis, which was a place that existed between both realms. She had discovered it not long after her own mysterious arrival.

Valeressa had not been escorted through the vortex by a watcher, rather she was found wandering through the realm on her own, lost and confused. She had no memory of her life in the other realm, though surely, she must have come from there. Master Burdock could not find her in the web, so he theorized that her attachments had been severed, and she had somehow willed herself into the watcher's realm, for he had not felt her alteration either.

Valeressa had learned much about her new existence. In the watcher's realm there were no more physical desires or needs – no hunger, no thirst, no fatigue. The innate desires for intimacy were satisfied in the familial relations with other watchers and with their interaction with the web itself. Other watchers were completely fulfilled by the love and acceptance they felt in this realm. For many, it was the first time they had ever felt the feelings associated with family and friendship. When they altered, each individual was offered the chance to change his or her name as a symbolic gesture of his or her transformation. Many chose names with special meanings, such as Haven (safe place), Akemi (dawn), or Lali (well-spoken).

Master Burdock had chosen the name Valeressa for her. He had told her that he had once known a woman with the same name who brought light to others, so she accepted the name, hoping she could embrace the former owner's qualities to give her some sense of purpose in her new surroundings.

The more time she spent around the other watchers, however, the more she realized that she was different. She appeared to be the oldest of the watchers who had altered. Most of them were under twenty, but her features and maturity set her age in her mid to late twenties. The emptiness in Valeressa's heart was merely obscured by her attachments to the others rather than filled by their presence, though they felt strongly attached to her. She was the one they sought out to discuss their feelings and experiences from their past lives. Many counseled with her before committing to a new name. She was known for her listening ear and her ability to put others at ease.

The place she felt most at home was in stasis. She was at peace there in the place where both realms collided. She had found it quite by accident. Because of the unusual nature of her appearance in the watcher's realm, she had not been permitted to watch in the other realm for quite some time. When she was finally given the opportunity, Master Burdock himself escorted her through the vortex. The experience had not gone well. She was not as attuned to the vibrations of the web as she should have been, and she found the experience exhausting.

Master Burdock was baffled, but he insisted that she could learn to feel the vibrations, so he took her out a second time, which proved to be disastrous when she discovered that she had retained the ability to touch in the other realm. No other watcher could do that. Master Burdock had been standing in front of a door as if waiting to enter a building, and Valeressa had instinctively reached out to open the door. The onlookers who belonged to the other realm were stunned to see a door open by itself with no hint of a breeze in the vicinity. Master Burdock had been perplexed enough that Valeressa had not been permitted to enter the other realm since.

On their return from her second visit, she was walking through the vortex beside Master Burdock when a grayish blur appeared. She tried to ignore it, but the blur seemed to follow her, beckoning for her to cross its threshold. She could not resist its pull, and thus she discovered stasis. Master Burdock had been alarmed for she had simply disappeared right in front of his eyes and did not reappear until much later when she finally decided to leave stasis to return to the watcher's realm.

Master Burdock had greeted her, worry lines creasing his forehead. When she explained what had happened, he listened intently as he stroked his goatee, the worry lines deepening. Then, he relaxed as if nothing out of the ordinary had happened at all. He explained to her his theory that she had found the place that held the two realms together, that she had a special gift since even he could not see her when she was in stasis. She could be truly invisible in both realms. He did not elaborate, though she often suspected he knew more than he told her. She understood that she was to discover those truths on her own.

***

Valeressa had just emerged from stasis, where she had gone for a short respite, when she heard someone approaching from behind her.

"Listen to me; I'm Minnion the Magnificent. I've never met her myself, but the other watchers say she has a way about her – an aura, some say."

She turned to see who accompanied him, but as she looked over her shoulder in their direction, a face forced its way into her mind. She closed her eyes. The face seemed familiar, ruggedly handsome with short brown hair and startling green eyes that stared at her longingly.

"Valeressa?" Minnion asked. As she opened her eyes, the face retreated from her memory though she tried to hold it in her view. She turned around to face the watchers who had sought her out. Valeressa noticed that Minnion looked at her strangely before abruptly leaving. She knew that Minnion was the watcher who had helped the boy called Kaleb to alter, though she had never met him before. She looked to his companion who stood in front of her, alone. She had seen his body every day in stasis for three years, keeping careful watch over him, and now here he was before her. Why had he sought her out?

"Strange," she said, "Is your watcher all right?"

"Who? Minnion? I suppose so. He seemed fine a minute ago. Are you all right?" No wonder Minnion had looked at her with such an expression. He had not been privy

to her little vision, and she must have appeared very unsettled to him.

"Yes, of course. I was clearing my mind, that's all. Now, how may I be of assistance to you?" She gestured for him to sit.

"Well…you know…" he shook his head, unable to say what he had come to discuss. "This is ridiculous. I'm sorry I wasted your time."

"No time is wasted, Kaleb." The name sounded strange leaving her own lips. She had never spoken his name before, though she kept a silent watch over him every day. She thought it curious that he had retained his name from the other realm, rather than fully embracing his new life as a watcher. Yet, she also knew that the link holding him to the other realm was far stronger and far more real than he knew.

"You know my name?" She smiled gently at him, and he immediately felt at ease.

"Yes, Kaleb. I know you've had a difficult time adjusting these past few years, but you've done remarkably well."

"But how do you know all that?" he wondered aloud.

"Master Burdock thought you might come to see me one day." She did not like lying to a fellow watcher, and she hoped he could not sense her deception. She did not know how keen his senses were in this realm, but he seemed content with her answer.

"What troubles you? I sense there is something weighing on your mind."

"Well, there's this girl," he said. So, he had found her. Valeressa listened with increased interest. "What I mean to say is . . . well . . . have you ever formed an attachment to someone you watched? I mean, for three years she could not see me, but I watched her still because the web directed me to her even when I knew she couldn't see me. I wonder if that's ever happened before."

"I cannot answer that for I serve a different role here. I'm an exception, though the secret to my past no one knows, thus I am not allowed in the other realm. I watch after the watchers instead."

"Do you think there is there something wrong with me?"

"Of course, there's nothing wrong with you, Kaleb," she paused for a moment. "She

still can't see you?"

"This week. Jessie saw me for the first time this week."

"And?"

"Well, I didn't feel the same as I do when I approach others. I was relieved that she could finally see me. I wanted her to know about me. I told her about myself, not because I had to, but because I wanted to. I didn't want her to believe me – to alter right away – because I want to spend more time with her. I want to talk to her, and I find myself looking forward to seeing her and spending time with her. That's not normal."

"It's natural for you to feel attachments, Kaleb. You're part of the web, if only on its periphery. You feel connections to other watchers, don't you? Minnion, perhaps?"

"Of course, but this seems different," he argued.

"Only because she's still in the other realm, and you said you have been watching her for a while. Might I suggest that you enjoy your time with her? Maybe it will help to heal your heart fully and completely as I sense that you have not yet fully embraced all that the watcher's realm has to offer. Maybe this is what you need," Valeressa tried to assuage his fears while urging him forward with sound logic. She did not want to interfere with his decision. This had to be his choice, but she felt that a little encouragement in the right direction could certainly do no harm. Kaleb smiled at her. She had succeeded.

"Thank you, Valeressa. The other watchers are right about you – you do have a way about you. I'm glad someone is here to watch out for us watchers."

"I do try to serve my purpose just as you do. Feel free to stop by and talk whenever. I'm always here."

"I'll do that," he assured her as he stood to leave.

"And Kaleb, it's okay to follow your heart, even as a watcher. That's how Minnion came to save you, after all." He nodded his head and went on his way, probably back to the other realm if her suspicions were correct. She smiled to herself, and then felt an unexpected surge of loneliness rush through her. She realized that she had been subconsciously searching for the image that had manifested itself to her when Minnion and

Kaleb had approached. Did Kaleb have something to do with its mysterious appearance and subsequent disappearance?

Chapter 3: My Beginning

My Beginning

His blonde hair and blue eyes,
His black shirt and Levis,
His boyish charm and distinguished smile,
His sense of a more matured style,
His tender gaze in my direction,
His kind gestures, a subtle affection?
His interest and common traits,
His presence was worth the wait.
His choice of me among the rest,
He makes me feel my very best.
My love for him is undenied,
For only in him can I confide.
And as he disappears each night,
I am overcome with my constant fright,
He may be leaving in another day,
He soon may be too far away.
But still, I watch with one last glimpse,
Of Kaleb, my first true charming prince.

~ Jessie Watson

The next day at school, Jessie spent her lunch hour in the hallway completing her homework because she didn't want to spend all of her time with Kaleb working on calculus. After school, Jessie walked with a quicker pace toward the park. Kaleb was there, sitting on the bench of her table, watching for her.

"Hey," he called as she approached him, "what's on the docket for today?"

"Whatever you want," she answered.

"What do you mean? No calculus to torture me with?"

"I finished the homework already, thanks to a great tutor. I was hoping we could just talk, if that's okay?"

"Fine with me. What do you want to talk about?" he asked curiously.

"Tell me more about yourself," she said.

"You already know everything you need to know about me." He was watching her with interest.

"No. I only know about the lowest point of your life. What was your life like before that?" she asked.

"It was a normal life as far as I knew. I hung out with my friends playing basketball and stuff. I was a regular teenager – nothing special about me. Now you, that's another story," he said, deflecting her question.

"What do you mean by that?" she asked breaking her eye contact. "There's nothing to my story."

"That's where you're wrong, Jessie," he paused as he moved, so her eyes would meet his again, "your life is so riddled with holes and sadness, and yet here you are, trudging along as if you were like everyone else, but you aren't like them, are you? You are stronger…fiercer…because most people would have buckled under the load you carry. They would have given up the fight."

"Thanks…I think. I'm not really sure what you're getting at, Kaleb. I have no choice. My life is what it is, and I'm kind of stuck with it."

"You don't understand. You aren't like other people, even other foster kids that I've met who are in similar circumstances. How can I explain this to you? Well, take your poetry for instance…You have one poem in particular that demonstrates my point, if you'll indulge me," he said smiling. He didn't wait for any more objections before he began:

"Happiness is the sun that spreads its rays of brightness and warmth
around us.
Love is the mountain range that stands as a quiet protection and
security.
Hope is the wide expanse of sky that blankets each night and day.
Comfort is the ocean that takes out the tide of confusion and sorrow.
Peace is the earth ~ the soil that is forever trodden upon by the feet
of war but uncovered by the bonds of friendship.
Mistakes are the clouds that are present at times in the sky of hope
and occasionally hide the sun of happiness.
Forgiveness is the moon and stars that dot the darkness and absence,
yet bring new light until the sun awakens.
A smile is the flower garden that envelops the world with beauty and
pleasure.
Laughter is the cool breeze that blows the devastating heat away.
Service is the thunder that awakens the tired and the weak."

She was dumbstruck. He quoted her poem word for word, seemingly impressed by the ideas the words conveyed. She didn't understand it.

"You have it memorized?" she asked.

"Being a watcher has its perks," he simply replied, "but you're missing the point. Jessie, it took me becoming a watcher before I understood what you already know. You write so poignantly about concepts that are as unfamiliar to you as a foreign language. You write with hope when your dreams are constantly breaking before your eyes. I've met so many people in your situation who alter at very young ages because they completely lose their hope. But you…you hang on.

"When the web first directed me to be your watcher, I pitied you. My heart broke for you like it does for everyone else. As time went on, my pity turned to admiration. You dug in your heels, built your wall to protect yourself, and you kept going. What's more fascinating is that you don't seem to hate anyone for it. You place the blame squarely upon your shoulders, where it doesn't belong. Hate was the first emotion I felt when my parents died."

Her face was turning red. She was embarrassed that he seemed to be idolizing her. What was she, some kind of superhero among the forgotten? The silence soon gave way to the distant sound of sirens.

"Kaleb, you're not describing me. I've got a whole tablet full of darker poetry as well. I've got plenty of bitterness locked up inside of me too. I'm not some kind of heroine or whoever it is you think I am."

"Yeah, but you always find the light. I've seen you smiling to yourself when there's no reason to smile. I've seen you laughing when you're all alone. I've seen you crying bitter tears of disappointment too, but you have found the intricate balance between the light and the dark."

"Well, it doesn't feel like that," she interrupted him again. She admittedly was not a very good listener; she lacked the experience.

"Do you remember when you were staying with the Robinson's and a brand-new baby was placed with them?" he asked. She got the chills as he spoke. It was disconcerting to think that he knew so much about her. She nodded her head in agreement.

"It was a few weeks after your Heart-to-Heart bit aired on the local news. You were pretty much at the end of your rope from what I could tell. You seemed to be waiting for the unseen executioner to pull the trigger on your life. Yet you came home from school one day to find Mrs. Robinson at her wits end. The baby had been crying all day, and she couldn't handle it anymore. Without saying a word, you picked up the baby and started rocking him, singing him a lullaby. You were singing to him 'Learn to Be Lonely.'

"When he heard the sound of your voice, he calmed down and eventually went to sleep. It's as if somehow, he knew you were his advocate. Though you told him he would be alone, he knew you didn't believe it – you had hope for him. While your world was shattering, you were putting his together for him. Then there was the time that Ashley's adoption fell through when you were with the Hendricks' family. Who was there cracking jokes and trying to lift her spirits? You. And who remembered Trever's birthday when everyone else forgot? You. And then there was prom. I mentioned that before, but I saw what happened after you drained all your tears. You got up, curtsied, smiled – a smile I will never forget – and you danced in the moonlight by yourself…smiling when you had no reason to smile," he concluded his passionate soliloquy.

Jessie had never thought much of those insignificant moments. She was touched that Kaleb had taken note of them. He really did know her, everything about her, and he wasn't repulsed. He didn't think she was a depressed pessimist; instead, he admired the depth of her feelings. He admired the little flecks of hope she clung to – those little bits of hope that forced her eyes to open every morning, embracing the new day instead of damning it. Her life somehow gave meaning to his, even though he was a watcher.

She felt happiness bubbling up inside like a fresh spring breaking through the earth's surface. Even now, he waited patiently for her to gather her thoughts. He didn't try to rush her into a response. He was content to watch her as she entered her own private realm to think, and he watched tenderly as she processed emotions she had never felt before. A slow smile spread across her face.

"No one has ever said things like that to me. Thank you," she said as she noticed the sky had darkened enough to let the first few stars of the night peek through its black curtain. She started walking toward the house, intending to wave goodbye to Kaleb again, when she realized that he wasn't sitting at the picnic table. He was walking beside her with his hands in his pockets, but she knew that he was beside her before she ever turned to look. She felt as if someone had draped a security blanket over her shoulders to protect her from the cold.

He winked at her as their eyes met, and he walked with her all the way to the door before she whispered goodbye. That was the first time in her life her silent walk home filled her with rapture rather than sadness. The silence of his presence seemed to seep into the holes in her heart, filling them with love and acceptance. For two nights in a row, she slept soundly.

Over the course of the next few weeks, she often spent time at the park talking to Kaleb. Eventually, she persuaded the ever-evasive Kaleb to talk to her about the memories he had of his happy childhood – memories that had been buried for far too long. She watched as his eyes danced with excitement as he described his favorite boyhood toy: his big yellow Tonka truck. She laughed when he told her about the time he cut the hair off of his mother's favorite porcelain doll because he thought the cat needed a moustache. She listened longingly as he described his mom's homemade apple pie, which was hot and ready every Sunday evening. He talked of how his dad taught him to play the guitar, and she wished he could play it for her now. She couldn't help but feel envious of him, but sad at the same time at what he had become.

One afternoon Jessie dropped by the house before going to the park to meet Kaleb. On her bed, she found a letter from the local university. She was surprised to receive a letter so soon. She picked up the envelope on her way out, shuffling it in her hands.

"What do you have there?" Kaleb asked as she approached.

"My future…the reply to my college application."

"Why don't you open it?"

"I'm nervous. What if I didn't get accepted?"

"Who knows if you'll still be around by then," Kaleb said indifferently. Jessie shot him a disapproving look.

"Hey, I'm just saying…but you know that's why I'm here, right?" he reminded her.

"I was trying to forget. My life seemed semi-normal for a while," she acknowledged.

"What do you mean by that?"

"Well…never mind…you wouldn't understand," Jessie wasn't about to own up to the fact that Kaleb had brought her out of her slump.

"Jessie, you have every right to a normal life. I'm not trying to take that away from you. I don't cause this to happen to people –"

Jessie cut him off before he could finish, "That's not what I meant, Kaleb. My life seems more normal since I met you than it did before. How messed up is that? I'm happier since my imaginary friend showed up," she finally confessed.

"That's not so hard to understand. We're a lot alike…go ahead and open it," he said pointing to the envelope, which Jessie had set on the picnic table. Her fingers stiffened with nerves, so she could hardly get the envelope opened. She carefully pulled out the letter and read its contents – a smile erupting on her face like fireworks on the Fourth of July.

"I take it you got in?" Kaleb said with a small smile of his own.

"I not only got in, but I got a four-year, academic scholarship that will pay for my tuition!" she exclaimed as she reread the letter to make sure she hadn't missed anything.

"Congratulations, Jessie! Your hard work just paid off," Kaleb commented, but Jessie detected a hint of sadness in his voice.

"Are you okay?" she asked, worried that she had somehow upset him.

"Jessie, why don't you be happy for you and quit worrying about me? I didn't mean to detract from your news. I'm really excited for you," he explained.

"Then what's wrong?" she persisted.

"My mom worked for the university, and your acceptance there reminded me of her, that's all," he said. Noting her surprise at his comment, he clarified, "Jessie, being a watcher didn't erase my emotions – it merely gave me a sense of purpose. Of course, with my new understanding of the world, I have been able overcome the hate and anger I once felt about the accident, but that took time. I still get angry every now and again, and the sadness is still a part of my life – it will always be a part of who I am because I'm still the same Kaleb Scott that I was before. Well, a more enlightened and controlled version of myself."

"I'm sorry…I didn't know…I didn't understand…" she stammered somberly, feeling as though her little fireworks show had burned new holes in Kaleb's heart.

"Don't be sorry for me, Jessie. I'm fine. You know that's one thing that continues to draw me toward you the more time I spend with you," he said thoughtfully.

"What?" wondered Jessie, confused.

"Most people would have been too wrapped up in the excitement of the moment just now to notice how I was feeling. Most people I meet are too wrapped up in themselves to notice me at all, even as a watcher, even when they can see me. Not you…you make me feel at ease, and you always seem to know exactly how I'm feeling no matter how hard I try to disguise it," he stated.

"It's funny you should think that of me when that's exactly how I feel about you," she noted as she stared into his beautiful eyes, her mind adrift in his ocean of blue. Silence followed as they looked at each other, lost in their own thoughts, completely unaware that their breathing increased in tandem. Under normal circumstances, Jessie would have been unable to maintain eye contact for that long without becoming uncomfortable and self-conscious, but now she was so mesmerized by him that she could not look away from him. She finally spoke, "So, what did your mom do at the university?"

"She was a botany professor, well an adjunct professor technically. She taught a few labs and undergrad classes every semester. She was obsessed with plants and nature, and she loved teaching about it. I think she was planning to recreate the Garden of Eden in her own backyard once my parents built their dream house. That's one reason I liked the poem I quoted the other night. It compared the attributes I was supposed to acquire as a watcher to nature. It merged my two worlds into one…listen to me ramble on," he interrupted his own thoughts, which disappointed Jessie because she loved to listen to him as he strolled down memory lane. His eyes seemed more alive as he spoke of his past, and she never grew weary of hearing about his life. The stories became a part of her, and for the first time, she felt as though she actually belonged to his family in a strange but familiar way.

"I like to hear you reminisce," she reassured him, "I wouldn't ask if I wasn't interested. So, were you going to attend the university as well before you altered?"

"Oh, heck no," the abruptness of his reply startled her, and observing her surprise, he went on, "Don't get me wrong. I loved my parents, but we had our difficulties and differences of opinion. I certainly wasn't a saint for a son. My parents were sometimes overbearing, and I didn't want my mom constantly checking up on me and talking to my professors. No way. I was bent on going out of state, as far away as possible. I had a scholarship to go to an Ivy League college back east. I all but had my bags packed to leave and experience life on my own – freedom. Ironic, isn't it? I got what I wanted – it just wasn't the freedom I was expecting. It turned out to be a one-way ticket to the Land of No Return." Jessie had never seen this side of Kaleb before. He always idolized his parents whenever he mentioned them. She assumed he had the perfect family life. Maybe the perfect family didn't exist outside of her head. The perfect family was one who exhibited tolerance for the weaknesses of the others and learned to love each other in spite of them.

"And here I thought you were perfect," she tried to lighten the sullen mood her question had evoked.

"You've heard the adage: The grass is always greener on the other side of the fence. I think it's like that for everyone. You never appreciate what you have until it's been taken from you – until it's too late to appreciate it," he pointed out.

"True enough," she said, trying unsuccessfully to convince herself that her grass was green enough.

"So, have you visited the campus?" he asked. Jessie was grateful for the distraction from her present line of thought, which had withered all the grass in the entire neighborhood.

"No, I didn't want to go by myself, but I wasn't sure if I wanted to go with Mrs. Moore either. She's my only other alternative," she responded.

"Why don't you go with me? I can give you a personal tour. I know the campus like the back of my hand, and you won't be embarrassed by having to drag an adult along – you'll be inconspicuous just as you like," he laughed.

"Really? That would be so great, but only if you're as good at tours as you are at tutoring," she said. "When do you want to go?"

"We can go tomorrow after school if you don't have too much homework," he replied.

"Sure, and speaking of homework, I have a bunch to do tonight," she remembered her heavy backpack awaiting her at the house.

"Let me walk you home then, so you can get to it," he said. Sometimes he hung around, helping her every now and again if she had a question, and sometimes he left.

"Do you have somewhere to be tonight?" she asked. She wasn't quite ready for him to leave yet.

"Not in particular,' he answered.

"Are you bored out of your mind most of the time, just waiting?" she asked with dismay.

"Time doesn't really work that way in this realm. I always have responsibilities to perform, and people to watch out for. There's really no room for boredom. If I'm not with you, there are plenty of other strands to occupy my time," he clarified. She couldn't quite grasp the concept of time he was trying to explain, but she didn't want him to know that, so she nodded her head as though she understood.

"You're not fooling anyone, Jessie," he laughed, "you haven't got a clue what I'm talking about, do you?"

She felt her face flush as she admitted, "You've got me there."

"You don't have to leave, you know," she said as they approached the door, "I might need my calculus tutor." He raised an eyebrow, but followed her into the house. Dinner was ready when she walked in, so she sat down to eat while Kaleb waited, watching her as he appeared to lean against the dining room wall.

"So?" Mrs. Moore asked, "Have you heard from the university?" Mealtimes were generally quiet at the Moore household, since Jessie wasn't much of a conversationalist. When she was asked about her day, she gave only one-word responses. She typically ate quickly, helped with the dishes, and retired to her room where she stayed until the following morning. Jessie felt awkward now.

"Yeah, I got in," she said casually. Jessie kept her distance from people, and the Moore's were no exception. She had learned to live a life without praise and acceptance; therefore, she didn't expect it from anyone.

"Congratulations, Jessie! We're so happy for you," Mrs. Moore's genuine tone invited Jessie to divulge more information than she might normally have done. Maybe a little praise wouldn't hurt her after all.

"I was awarded a scholarship, too – full tuition for four years," she announced proudly. She had worked hard for that scholarship. She spent most of her solitary life consumed with studying. It was all she had that would save her from being a nobody in a somebody's world. She wouldn't reject any praise for that. She deserved at least that much recognition. Mrs. Moore unexpectedly leaped out of her chair, coming around the table to hug Jessie. Jessie was stunned by the sudden movement – she hadn't been expecting this kind of public display. Kaleb watched Jessie's reaction with interest. She only half-heartedly hugged Mrs. Moore as her face turned beet red. She wasn't used to physical contact, and she seemed uncomfortable in the spotlight, even if it was only Mrs. Moore's spotlight.

"Oh, we're so proud of you," Mrs. Moore commended Jessie as she returned to her seat. Mr. Moore nodded in agreement, though he said nothing. He was a quiet man who rarely spoke in Jessie's presence. He was content to let his wife be the mouthpiece and dominant partner in the relationship.

"Thanks," Jessie said as she cleared her plate from the table. "I have a lot of homework tonight. Do you mind if I head up to my room?" She didn't usually ask for permission to go to her room, but tonight, she was trying to excuse herself from helping with the dishes.

"Sure. Sure. Go ahead," came Mrs. Moore's pleasant reply.

Jessie sat down on the bed when she got to her room and began pulling her books from her bursting backpack. Kaleb sat beside her.

"I didn't know a person's face could get that red," Kaleb smirked.

"Shut up, Kaleb," she said as she reflexively reached out to punch him in the arm. Her hand kept going when it should have pounded into flesh, plowing into the wall instead. She gasped in shock while shaking her throbbing knuckles and stared at him in astonishment as the wave of realization spread over her. He really was invisible. She couldn't touch him. He couldn't touch her. He couldn't touch anything. He seemed to shrug it off, choosing to ignore her puzzled expression.

"Nice try. It serves you right for trying to punch me," Kaleb chuckled, putting his hands behind his head, appearing to lean against the headboard, "now let's get to work." Jessie obediently opened her book and pulled out the worksheet she was assigned. Subject by subject, she completed her homework while Kaleb kept her company, offering assistance when asked, discussing at length her literature essay, and watching silently as she read her assigned chapters. When it came time to study for her U.S. Government test, Kaleb quizzed her relentlessly until she knew the material forward and backward.

"Well, that does it for tonight. Thanks for your help. I still maintain that you must be pretty bored if you're hanging out here with me helping me with high school courses, time continuum or not," she noted.

He shook his head in response, "See you tomorrow, Jessie. Goodnight, sleep tight, don't let the bed bugs bite. Mom used to say that to me when I was a kid," he recalled as he disappeared through the door. Unbeknownst to him, Kaleb reappeared in Jessie's dreams that night.

Luckily, the next afternoon, Jessie had very little homework. The day was perfect for a campus visit with the sun shining its approval on her afternoon plans with Kaleb. Mrs. Moore hadn't objected either, though she tried to persuade Jessie not to go by herself. She assured Mrs. Moore that she would be back before dark, and finally Mrs. Moore relented. Jessie met Kaleb at the park, and they walked to the bus stop with Jessie chattering happily about doing well on her history test, thanks to Kaleb. They sat in silence on the bus ride. Jessie would have looked absurd talking to herself all the way to the university.

The university had a sprawling campus, divided into an upper and lower region. Jessie felt like a small ant among hundreds in a manmade ant farm. Kaleb began by showing her the student union building, which was a three-story building that housed the food court, several computer labs and conference rooms, the university bookstore, the campus theater, and a recreational area, complete with a bowling alley and game room. He then took her to the living and learning center, where the dorm students not only lived, but also took most of their classes. They toured all of the buildings of the various departments. Campus was a maze of buildings, parking, sports and fitness facilities, and open spaces. Without Kaleb as a guide, she would have been lost within the first few minutes of setting foot on the sidewalk.

Her favorite building was the library, which felt like an ancient enchanted castle, musty smell and all. Her footsteps echoed as she climbed the spiral staircase. She was very aware that hers were the only footsteps she heard, though Kaleb was right beside her telling her about the time he had gotten lost in the library.

"I wandered off, pretending I was a famous explorer who had found the ruins of an ancient city. It took at least an hour of frantic searching by my mom, who had enlisted the help of several of her students, as well as the library staff," he remembered.

"Where did they find you?"

"I had fallen asleep in the microfiche section downstairs in the basement. My mom was livid when she finally found me. I wasn't allowed to come to the library after that without a harness attached to me, which was quite the humiliation for an eight-year-old boy," he recalled, laughing.

"I hope I'm not boring you to death," he said as he turned to look at her.

"Actually, I feel jealous of you," she remarked honestly, "but I love to hear your stories because they're about you, and somehow I feel as though I experience them with you as you tell me about them – so they become a part of me too. Isn't that psychotic?"

"A little flattering actually – that you would want to be a part of my life, yet sad that you have to experience life through someone else, especially if that someone else is me," he said. "There's so much more I wish I could give you, but I can't."

"Like what?" she inquired.

"I wish I could show you how to play golf in your P.E. class. I would teach you how to grip the club and swing at the right angle so you can actually hit the ball off the tee for once," he joked.

"You stay out of my P.E. class. You're officially banned! Besides, I'm not bad at every sport I try. I won third place in the badminton tournament, or did you miss that one?" she quipped back, although another part of her mind was visualizing Kaleb standing behind her with his arms around her as he showed her how to grip a golf club. She imagined his smell, his breath in her ear as he gave her instructions, his arms – strong and firm – cradling her, his hands over her own. Yes, she wished he could teach her that too.

"No, you would be a worthy badminton opponent," he agreed, her dream evaporating with his words. Her stomach grumbled all too loudly, announcing its hunger to the entire library.

"Sounds like I'd better get you back. It's past dinnertime," he surmised, but Jessie was reluctant to go. She wanted to linger here a little longer in his presence. Just then, a group of college students entered the library, bumping into her without an apology or an excuse me, as if she was invisible like Kaleb. It was the little nudge she needed back to reality – her reality – a reality where Kaleb couldn't be seen by anyone but her.

"Thanks for the tour," she said as she bid him goodnight at the bus stop. As Jessie rode home, alone on the bus, she committed the afternoon to her memory, retracing their steps in her head, reliving each moment, each look, each laugh, and each story. She never wanted to forget this afternoon or any moment she spent with Kaleb because she didn't know how many more afternoons she would have with him. She didn't know how long this was going to last or how her story would end.

***

Jessie was happy to find that her time with Kaleb had not yet drawn to an end. She continued to spend her afternoons and some evenings with him, much as before. One Friday in particular, she mustered up enough courage to ask him the question that had been on her mind since the first time they had met.

"Kaleb, can you come back once you've altered?"

"I've never heard of that happening before. Most people are happier as watchers than they've ever been before."

"Most people. You said most people, but what about you?"

"Well, I told you before. I'm not like most watchers. It's true that I'm happier here than I once was when I was consumed by rage and grief."

"But," she said, noting that he was once again surprised by her perceptiveness in reading his feelings.

"But...sometimes meeting someone has a way of changing how a person views happiness...maybe having a sense of purpose isn't enough anymore." He seemed to be thinking out loud and caught himself before he revealed too much, "But none of that matters. I am what I am. Once a person alters, there is no way back. I made my decision a long time ago, and I'm grateful for the chance I've had to see the world as it was meant to be seen and to help people...especially people like you."

"How long have you been like this?"

"Not long, maybe a couple of years at the most. I lose track of time. Remember, time doesn't have much meaning in my realm as a watcher."

"What is it like in your realm? Do you wander around aimlessly by yourself?" she inquired.

"I can't describe what it's like here in a way you would understand. In this realm, I do watch the web by myself, but I don't wander aimlessly. I'm given assignments on occasion, and I find broken strands on my own as the web guides me. In the other realm, I'm with the other watchers. We have a brotherhood and a sisterhood if I could describe it like that. I have a special bond with the watcher who helped me alter, but we all kind of draw strength from each other and the web. Does that make any sense?" he wondered.

"Kind of," she said hesitantly.

"You're afraid of being alone after you alter?" he asked, guessing part of her uncertainty.

"Yes, partly, but what happens to you and me? Do we still get to talk?"

"Well, not in the sense you may be thinking. It's different in the other realm. We would become fellow watchers, and we would go about our separate duties as watchers. We would still bump into each other, but it would be…well…different. I would never forget you, Jessie, if that's what you're thinking," he tried to reassure her, but he guessed wrong this time. She wasn't worried he would forget her; she was worried that she would forget him. She had so naturally and easily fallen in love with him, almost without realizing it. She didn't want to lose this feeling, even if it meant being alone forever.

He seemed to catch himself in his mistake as he quickly added, "Jessie, don't do anything stupid, okay? Altering is serious business – don't think you'll get to spend more time with me because it doesn't work like that in the watcher's realm." *But I would follow you there if it did work like that*, she thought, *I would follow you into the unknown if it meant I could be with you.*

He looked at her intently, apparently debating with himself. After a few moments of silence and contemplation, he said, "Jessie, I probably shouldn't do this, but I'm going to anyway. What's youth without a little reckless abandon, even for a watcher?" She eyed him quizzically.

"I want you to come somewhere with me tomorrow – to a place I've never shown anyone before. Will you…will you come with me?" he asked.

"Okay," she agreed, "where are we going?'

"Home," he said quietly.

"Home?"

"Yes, we're going to the place that should have been my home if death hadn't intervened and robbed me of it. My parents had saved up for years to be able to build their dream house on some property they owned outside of town and had just sold our house before they died. Since all of our stuff was already in storage on the property, we were staying in a furnished condo until the house was built. We are both homeless now in a sense – in between places – with no one but each other. Before you alter, I want you to know what home is, at least what it felt like for me," he explained.

***

Tomorrow couldn't come fast enough for Jessie. She dressed in a hurry, told Mrs. Moore that she would be at the library all day, and headed out the door. Kaleb was waiting for her by the tree. His property wasn't exactly near her foster house, and she didn't have any transportation. They had to rely on the city bus and then walk the rest of the distance. When they came over a small hill, she saw the most beautiful acreage. It overlooked the forest as if it were created to warn the valley below of any danger. Kaleb paused for a minute at the top of the hill before joining her below, a slow smile spreading on his face. She could tell he hadn't been here since he had altered, but it seemed to be a pleasant memory for him. She noticed the large barn like structure, which she assumed to be the storage area. That building seemed to fill its space naturally, as if it had grown there like the surrounding trees. They stood on top of the hill for a moment before Kaleb spoke.

"After I moved out of the condo and brought everything here, I never really felt homeless. I slept out here under the stars every night, and somehow, I felt closer to my parents, closer to that life of happiness I once knew. I would listen to the owls hoot in the trees, knowing that I belonged here in this spot just as they did. I felt as though this place had been created for me, with the trees standing guard against the intruding loneliness like giant sentinels – the dirt road making it more difficult for hatred to kidnap the only peace I had left. I would look up at the stars, seeing a thousand twinkling lights like the thousand I love you's my parents whispered into my ear each night when they thought I was asleep. I could hear the leaves rustling in the trees, and a hundred happy memories of camping trips and hiking excursions filled my emptiness. When the breeze blew it was as though my parents were embracing me one last time beyond their graves. I stayed out here for an entire month, completely secluded before I gave into the hate and pain. My mighty fortress caved in on me," he revealed his feelings so zealously that she was swept away into his vision. She felt as though she was there beside him, experiencing all his emotions with him. She didn't want to interrupt the mood he had set, so she said nothing.

"When I was new to this realm, right after I altered, I didn't yet grasp the concept of my purpose. I was different from other watchers because I had left a life behind that had once been filled with hope and promise. I struggled. The pain was still so fresh, my wounds unhealed. As I watched you, I slowly began to understand why the world was worth saving. I saw your hope, your goodness, and the idea of love you embraced though it had been denied you."

"You've got me confused with someone else again," she interrupted.

"No, I don't. Seriously, you have a great sense of humor. Do you remember the time you put the plastic bugs in Jack's bed when you were at the Tilly's house?"

She snickered at the memory, "Big, bad Jack. An eight-year-old menace to the Tilly household. How could I forget him? He was always tormenting the Tilly's kids. He told them he wasn't afraid of anything, but I knew otherwise. He screamed like a little girl that night, but at least he quit bothering the kids."

"Did you know that the Tilly's eventually adopted him?"

"No, I hadn't heard. Good for Jack. I'm glad things worked out for him," she answered with genuine congratulations in her tone.

"You had a hand in it. Without your little practical joke, he may never have been put in his place. He respected you," Kaleb interjected. Jessie hadn't seen Jack in a long time. She had almost forgotten about him, since she crossed paths with so many foster kids as she was moved around. She enjoyed reminiscing with Kaleb, and she was glad he was the one who knew everything about her.

"Anyway, as I was saying before I was interrupted. You weren't always this low, Jessie. That's only gradually happened since the Heart-to-Heart episode. The one thing that should have changed your life actually started destroying it. I saw you laugh in your loneliness, more so before, but I still catch glimpses now and again. I saw you light the way for others like Jack, completely oblivious to the warmth you were radiating. When you wrote that poem as if you'd written it just for me, I finally understood. I understood how the web worked. I understood that people were inherently good – they got distracted. I understood what the watchers had been trying to teach me. You taught me that, and you're not even a watcher yet," he finished the sentence, the last word barely audible as if he was reluctant to say it.

"Thanks for bringing me out here, Kaleb. I love it – it's beautiful and peaceful – the perfect escape," she lay down on the ground as she spoke to get a better view of the sky.

"I like to watch the clouds roll by. That's how I used to escape when I was little," she said as she watched a dragon float into view. He rested his ghostly form next to her, and they watched the world revolve slowly on its axis, documenting the passing time with the shifting clouds. Neither of them felt obligated to speak. They reveled in the silence, content to be in each other's presence. That was how Jessie had always imagined love. She felt as though they were magnets, their spirits drawn to each other by some inexplicable force – two people with so much in common and yet worlds apart. After a while, Kaleb broke the silence with the rich tones of his voice. She was surprised to feel her heartbeat quicken as he spoke her name.

"Jessie, I have something I want to show you," he said, getting up from the ground and heading down the hill. He paused halfway down to wait for her, so they could walk side by side. They walked to the barn, which looked more foreboding the closer they got. Its massive doors were chained and padlocked. The chains were spotted with rust as if they were willing to sacrifice their existence to the elements rather than reveal the secrets hidden within.

Kaleb approached the barn slowly, reaching up for the lock. She was surprised when he quickly withdrew his hand before touching the lock, as if some force field prevented him from getting too close to it.

"What's wrong?" she wondered out loud. He looked up at her, almost surprised to see her standing there. He was clearly immersed in his own thoughts, and he had a distant look on his face. Instead of answering her, he reached for her hand, as if he was reaching for some extra support from her to bolster him up as he unlocked his past. Her heart leapt, beating a little faster than it ought as his hand slowly moved closer to hers. At the moment their hands were to touch, she felt a faint puff of air glide over her skin where his hand should have been. He looked at her glumly as if he had just remembered that he was nothing more than the ghost of a person who no longer existed – a ghost who carried his burden alone, unable to share it with anyone.

"Looks like you'll have to do it," he muttered.

"Do what?" she asked, perplexed.

"Open the door, silly. I know where the key is, but I can't grab it." He laughed at her, but she didn't find the humor in the situation. She felt a pang of guilt for coming here in the first place, but she retrieved the key from its hiding place anyway and opened the lock. She pried open the doors and stepped back in awe of what she saw. The entire building was stacked high with dusty boxes and covered furniture. Kaleb's truck, a graduation present from his parents, was parked inside as well.

"Do you want to take her for a spin? If she starts, that is. She's been neglected for way too long." He was grinning again as he stared at the deep blue Toyota Tundra with that boyish grin that she had come to anticipate.

"What do you mean? I don't know how to drive!"

"I guess we'll see how good a teacher I am then," he mused. She had wished for this so many times over the past two years, but now she couldn't believe she was actually going to get behind the wheel to drive a vehicle. She opened the door to the truck, happy to see the keys still in the ignition from the last time he drove it. She was longing to touch something that he had touched before he altered. Over the past few weeks, he had become her truest friend. He was in fact the only friend she had ever had. She cherished the time they spent together. It was too bad he wasn't a real person, yet that was typical for her. Nothing ever seemed to work out in her favor.

"Jessie? You actually have to turn the key in the ignition to get it to go," he chuckled, rescuing her from her wandering thoughts. She turned the key, and the engine purred to life. She couldn't help but smile as she put the truck in reverse and instinctively pushed the gas.

"BRAKE!" screamed Kaleb. She came inches from hitting the tree that stood beside the barn. Her heart pounding, Kaleb coaxed her along the road. He assured her that no one would see her, but she couldn't help worrying that someone would report her driving a stolen truck. *Driving isn't too bad*, she thought to herself, just as Kaleb asked, "Jessie, what are you doing?"

"Duh, I'm driving," she smart-mouthed back to him.

"Why are you moving your hands back and forth like that? You've got to hold the wheel steady," he instructed.

"Well, that's how everyone pretends to drive. I thought…never mind," she withdrew her comment because it was sure to reveal how naive she really was. Kaleb was laughing in the passenger seat.

"I'm glad you're laughing at my expense!" she said, trying to concentrate on driving but stealing a glance in his direction.

"Oh, Jessie. You know I don't mean anything by it. You're so entertaining," he said, before being startled back to his assumed vocation as instructor. Jessie was headed straight off the road. Kaleb instinctively tried to reach for the steering wheel, but his hand whooshed right through it, as Jessie jerked it to the right and slammed on the brakes, bringing the truck to a screeching halt inches before hitting a fence post.

"Good heavens!" he exclaimed. He pretended to pat the dashboard with his hand as he said, "It's okay, baby. She didn't mean anything by it. You're okay."

"I'm done!" Jessie snapped at him, "I am so not touching your truck ever again." She hopped out of the driver's side in a huff. He was beside her before she could take a step forward.

"Come on, Jessie. You know I was only kidding with you," he reassured her while struggling to repress a laugh. She didn't budge. With her shaking arms folded across her chest, she turned her head in the opposite direction to avoid his penitent gaze.

"You can't leave it here. Someone will see it! And then there will be fingerprinting and questioning and possible jail time for trespassing," he let his voice trail off.

"Okay, okay, okay. Point taken, but if you're going to be my teacher, you've got to pay attention to the road!" she chided. Her heart beat had returned to its natural rhythm, and her hands weren't trembling as badly. She was able to maneuver the truck back to the barn, and Kaleb only once had to remind her to leave her left foot off the brake pedal since she kept trying to push the gas and the brake at the same time. With the truck safely parked, Jessie chained the doors to the barn shut and returned the padlock to its place.

"Will you forgive me?" Kaleb asked with child-like innocence as he batted his eyelids at her, looking as though he might cry.

"Of course. You let me drive your baby, didn't you? Besides, I could never stay mad at you for long. Thanks for the lesson. It was better than the horror stories I've heard coming out of the 'driver's dread' class. At least I'm not in tears," she said mockingly.

"If you only knew," he added with a wink.

Overall, the experience had been exhilarating. Jessie was reluctant to head back to the city, but the night once again publicized its arrival with its thick arm of blackness. After Kaleb walked with her to the bus stop, he said he had somewhere else he had to be, and it looked as though his mind was a million miles away. She rode the bus back alone, a tinge of regret tainting the happiness and warmth she felt in her heart. Why couldn't she have met

Kaleb under different circumstances? Weeks had passed, and she felt no closer to altering than the day she first saw him.

Something had changed though. Before, she trudged along in her mundane path of days, barely able to make it through the routines she called her life. She was filled with loneliness and fear. Since Kaleb had entered her life, she felt her loneliness dissipating. Every moment she spent with him, she felt closer and closer to him and yet farther and farther away. Before she met him, she was at least confident in the misery her life held for her. She expected no more, thus felt little grief over unmet expectations. Now, however, everything was different. She wasn't sure of anything anymore. Her bleak picture had been washed away like the surf washing over the sand, dislodging the individual grains and depositing them on a completely different island, a tropical paradise. If she wasn't about to alter, then how long would she be able to see him? How long could their friendship continue? What would happen if he became once again invisible to her? She couldn't bear the thought of living a single day without him by her side, sharing it with her.

Chapter 4: Chains of Strife

Chains of Strife

I want to run away, far away
The price is too high to pay
My heart is lost; my mind confused
My self-esteem has gone unused
My fears are too great to face
I can't keep up the pace
I see too many weaknesses - too much pain
I'm losing control; I think I'm insane
I pout my way through my distress
complaining about how my life is such a mess
I hate who I am and what I do
I hate to admit it, but it's all so true
I want to give up; I want to give in
I'm sick of being a prisoner of sin
I'm tired of feeling inferior day in and day out
I'm sick of always being depressed - moping about
But I don't know if I can break the chains of strife
because I've been suppressed by them all my life.
~ Jessie Watson

The following week seemed to fly by, but Jessie hadn't seen much of Kaleb. He seemed preoccupied, and she assumed he was helping someone else to alter into the watcher's realm. On Saturday morning, Jessie decided to go for a run. While she wasn't accustomed to running, she hoped the fresh air and exercise would help to clear her head. On her way home, she jogged by the park, secretly hoping to find Kaleb. As she approached, she recognized his familiar shape by the rusted slide that looked at the moment like the Leaning Tower of Pisa. She smiled as she neared him, but he didn't make eye contact with her.

"Is something wrong?" she asked him, trying to sound casual.

"Not really. I don't understand why you can see me if you aren't about ready to alter," the sound of his voice made her shiver.

She was taken back by his sudden interest in her altering. He hadn't mentioned taking her to the property in the few times she'd seen him since. She wondered what she had done wrong, and why he seemed to be withdrawing from her. After all, she wasn't sure if she wanted to alter. When she questioned him about altering, he deflected her inquires with the assurance that she wouldn't understand if he tried to explain, but everything would be okay. She could only imagine that he must be getting sick of hanging around her if nothing was going to happen.

Then, it finally donned on her: He was only spending time with her because it was his duty to do so. He never would have given her a second glance if he hadn't been a watcher. She had been so foolish to think otherwise. Hadn't she sealed off her heart long ago, so she couldn't be hurt by anyone? She struggled to keep her composure because she didn't want him to see how naive she had been. She didn't want him to see her cry. She mumbled a quick goodbye and turned away before he could respond.

Her vision was blurred from tears, which came swiftly now. She wanted to get back to her room, far away from anything and everyone. She wasn't paying attention as she rounded the corner and crossed the street. The next thing she knew, she was lying on the sidewalk with the wind knocked out of her. She looked around, but couldn't imagine what had knocked her down. She didn't see a car, and she hadn't heard any screeching tires. She didn't hear anything at all. Maybe she had altered. Her heart started to race, and she frantically searched for Kaleb. However, it wasn't Kaleb's eyes that met hers this time.

"Are you okay? I'm so sorry. I didn't see you there. It's like you came out of nowhere."

She recognized the voice immediately with sudden mortification. She had just plowed into none other than Shane Gunderson. Her tongue was tied, and she couldn't seem to speak.

"Are you hurt? I'm so sorry," he kept repeating. He appeared to be by himself, and she finally came to her senses.

"I'm okay. No need to apologize, it was my fault. I wasn't watching where I was going," she stared at the sidewalk as she spoke, not wanting to meet his concerned gaze. She moved to a sitting position, but her head was reeling.

"Can I help you get somewhere?" he asked with genuine concern.

"No, I live in the house across the street there. The yellow one. I can make it on my own. I just need a few minutes for my head to stop spinning," she assured him.

"Well, I can help you across the street at least. I really am sorry. I was out for my morning jog, and I was listening to some new tunes on my iPod. I wasn't paying attention either. By the way, my name is Shane Gunderson. I live in the house behind yours, so it looks like we're backyard neighbors," he rattled on, completely oblivious to the fact that Jessie's face had flushed a bright red color. She didn't want to admit that she already knew where he lived, the color of every shirt in his wardrobe, his favorite video games, and his preferred deodorant. She felt like a criminal sitting next to him. When she didn't answer, he continued trying to start a conversation.

"What's your name?" he queried.

"Oh, I'm sorry," she snapped back out of her thoughts, hoping not to slip up, revealing how much she actually did know about him, "my name is Jessie. Jessie Watson."

"How long have you lived in that house? I don't think I've seen you around before."

"Well, uh," she stammered, "I've only been there a couple of months. That's my foster home." As soon as the words escaped her lips, regret cartwheeled through her mind.

"That's cool," he replied, clearly not knowing what else to say. She had a way of making people uncomfortable. No wonder her strand was swaying in the breeze without attachments – she apparently only knew how to commit social suicide.

"Not really." *What am I doing now?* She berated herself. *Why can't I shut up and go into the house? Am I trying to make him feel like a complete idiot?* She had dreamed of having a conversation with Shane since the first time she noticed him in his bedroom window, and now she was completely obliterating her chances of keeping him as an acquaintance.

"Well, I guess you're right. That really sucks, doesn't it?" he chuckled at his own awkwardness. She managed to smile at his self-confidence, which seemed to be shielding him from her repellant comments. She could hardly believe he was still sitting next to her trying to initiate some kind of interaction.

"At least let me walk you to your door. You still seem a little shaken."

How could I not be shaken when I plowed into a rock of solid muscle? Her thoughts interrupted him, and she hadn't heard that last question he asked.

"What was that? I didn't catch your last question." She yearned for a cave to crawl into before she could say one more dumb thing in front of him.

"Oh, I asked if you were a senior because I haven't seen you at school before."

"Yeah. I'm a senior. We're actually in a lot of the same classes," she added. With that, his face reddened a little bit, but she wasn't apologizing for that.

"I guess I'm not very observant. You'd think I'd notice when a pretty new girl showed up in one of my classes. I'll have to keep an eye out for you." Her heart fluttered. Did he really just call her pretty? Seriously, he must have hit his head on the stop sign when she ran into him. He was either clearly delirious or incredibly suave or unnaturally polite. She ignored her reddened cheeks that were exposing her obvious discomfort, or was it pleasure?

"Yeah. I'll see you around. Thanks for lending me a hand across the street. I might have run into that parked car," she laughed at her own joke as she closed the door and breathed a heavy sigh, much to the wonderment of Mrs. Moore, who was peering at Jessie over the book she had been reading. Jessie said nothing in response to Mrs. Moore's quizzical looks, but continued up to her room, where she quietly shut the door and sat on her bed.

Jessie's encounter with Kaleb was nearly forgotten, as she replayed the last few minutes of her life. That one conversation was now definitely on her life's highlight reel, along with her driving lesson with Kaleb, or every minute she spent with Kaleb for that matter. For so long she had felt as though she was hindered by chains of strife that kept her spirit suppressed. Each link in that chain had been forged and strengthened over time as the result of not feeling loved, wanted, or needed. She hated herself and how inferior she felt around other people. She had withdrawn because of her lack of self-confidence, and she encased herself in a shell of shyness that not only seemed to keep her safe from heartache caused by others, but also ensured her a constant companion: loneliness.

At the moment though, she felt those chains slack. Shane hadn't made her feel inferior, and he seemed genuinely embarrassed that he hadn't noticed her at school. No one had ever asked beyond her name before, except for Kaleb, but then Kaleb already knew everything about her and rarely had to ask. Besides, Kaleb was invisible. Then, the thought struck her: Would she see Kaleb again if Shane's strand had somehow bonded to hers in genuine friendship? Was making an acquaintance enough to bond strands? Before she met Kaleb, she may not have spent the entire evening analyzing strands and bond attachments.

Jessie spent the rest of the day finishing up her literature composition at the library and didn't get home until after dark. She ate the dinner Mrs. Moore had prepared, helped with the clean-up, and retired to her room as usual. When she turned on her light, she glanced over at Shane's bedroom out of habit. She smiled to herself as she did a double take. Taped to his window was a type-written sign in a huge font that read, "Hi Jessie!" Shane's face was plastered against the window alongside it, waving. She waved back and then closed her blinds.

On the following Monday, Jessie didn't see Kaleb on the way to school, nor did she see him at school. She tried not to look for him, but she found herself constantly watching for him to appear. Shane was true to his word. He sought Jessie out in the first class they had together and asked her about her weekend. She complimented him on his sign-making abilities, and they shared a nice laugh and light conversation. She was amazed at how much difference one person made in the outlook of her entire day. She found that she didn't have to endure the entire day in long-suffering and silence. She looked forward to the classes she had with him, although she still hid at lunch time. The school day was over before she knew it.

On the way home, she hardly expected to see Kaleb at the tree, but there he was, apparently waiting for her. She couldn't read the expression on his face, but it certainly wasn't one of anger.

"So, where were you today? Missing in action? Tired of keeping an eye on me after all this time? Ready to move on to another subject?" She hadn't intended to sound rude, but she did have an edge to her voice. After all, her last encounter with Kaleb hadn't exactly been pleasant for her, but then again, it wasn't his fault she had developed feelings for him, feelings deeper than friendship.

"I shouldn't have been watching you as closely as I was before. That's all," he mumbled. "Although, I do see you've made some changes since I last saw you."

"I'm not sure what you're talking about," she said confused. Was he referring to Shane?

"You look different…happier," he acknowledged with a smirk.

"Well, I'm always happy to see you, of course, but I guess I am a different person since the last time I saw you. I have a friend who's actually in my own realm. I've never had a friend besides you in my entire life, but now someone actually notices that I exist," she explained.

"Really?" he looked perplexed.

"Yeah, Shane Gunderson. On my way home from the park, I accidentally ran into him. He's a really nice guy. He actually talked to me at school today." As he listened, Kaleb's face fell. Apparently, he hadn't been aware of her interaction with Shane, which surprised Jessie. He seemed a little jealous, perhaps.

"Ah yes, the one you peep at through your window when you think no one is looking," he divulged, clearly averting her attention away from himself.

"You know about that?" she remarked as her face flushed. She wished she had a rock to crawl under now, but Kaleb only smiled wryly at her.

"Hmmm. This is very interesting," he considered, seemingly still baffled by something. "Well, if anyone deserves it, Jessie, you do. I seemed to have upset you the last time we talked at the park. You left in such a hurry; I decided to give you some space. Like I said, I'm afraid I was watching too closely. I got a little too involved. Maybe I was presumptuous in assuming you would alter soon, but I can't figure it out. I don't understand why you can see me if you're not going to alter."

"So, maybe I'm forming bonds?" she offered.

"That's just it, Jessie. I can't see them. I can't feel them. Maybe…" his voice trailed off, and he was deep in thought. She didn't dare interrupt him, so she waited.

"Jessie!" Shane called to her as he approached from behind. She turned around quickly, wondering what he must be seeing: her…standing by a tree…talking to herself in hushed tones.

"Oh – hi, Shane." What was she supposed say? How was she supposed to explain? More awkward yet, Kaleb was still standing there, staring at her, half amused with the situation. Then, she noticed that Shane was not alone. He was accompanied by half a dozen other guys, not to mention Nikki. Jessie suddenly felt like a second-class citizen in their presence. She shrank back a little bit, stepping off the sidewalk like a scared school girl surrounded by bullies. Shane seemed to sense her discomfort.

"Are you on your way home?" he asked. The others in his group simply stared at her with either indifference, tolerance, curiosity, or a blend of all three. Feelings of inferiority began to surface as she resisted the urge to run away.

"Yeah," she confirmed as she stared at her shoes.

"We're headed that direction," he nodded in the direction of his house. "You can join us if you want." She hesitated, glancing sideways at Kaleb. He shook his head as an indication that she should accept the offer. *As if I need his permission,* she thought. On the other hand, she still felt bad for leaving him mid-conversation. For the first time since she'd met him, Kaleb seemed unsure of himself, and she wanted to know what was driving the sudden change in his composure. She shrugged at her last thought, which Shane interpreted as an affirmative response. Nikki let go of Shane's hand and moved in front of him, making room for Jessie to walk beside her.

"So, Shane tells us he lives in the house behind yours," Nikki stated.

"Yeah," Jessie replied uneasily. She had never been good at small talk.

"I'll bet you could tell us a few stories about Shane here, huh?" she laughed as she looked over her shoulder at Shane. Jessie was horrified. If Nikki only knew! She struggled to gather her thoughts enough to respond.

"Not much to tell, I'm afraid, but then again, I'm not very observant," she lied, hoping no one could tell how shaky her voice had become. Jessie was more than grateful to see the Moore's house, standing as a silent rescuer from her own social ineptness. While Nikki seemed friendly, Jessie was sure it was only because of Shane's coaxing. Jessie felt the invisible chains tighten around her momentary state of happiness. She could never break free. She couldn't be someone she was not. She was not like Nikki or Shane, and she was beginning to feel like Shane's "project." She found that she was no longer a big bundle of nerves around him, but his friends were a different story. She was no caterpillar tucked away safely in its chrysalis to emerge as a beautiful social butterfly at the enticement of a nice guy she had just met. She was a caterpillar tucked away safely in its chrysalis, protected from the outside, dying on the inside, never to emerge from the silence of its tomb.

Interlude 2

"Valeressa," the sound of her name lurched her from her thoughts, which seemed to be splintered into a million different pieces these days. "Do you have a minute?" It was Watcher Gage. She did not know him well, but she knew of him.

"Certainly," she assured him.

"I'm concerned about one of the other watchers," he said urgently.

"Oh?" Her calmness seemed to seep inside of him as well.

"It's Watcher Minnion. He's not acting like himself, and I think something is very wrong with him."

"What seems to be the matter?"

"He seems to be detaching himself from the rest of us, spending a lot of time by himself, watching less and less in the other realm. He doesn't seem as attuned to the web anymore. He's slipping."

"Why not go to Master Burdock if the problem is this serious?" she asked, but he looked away from her. "Gage?"

"I think it's my fault. No, I know it's entirely my fault," he confided, his voice shaky, his hands trembling. She did not push him. She simply waited until he was ready to talk. "You see, I was watching in the other realm one night – about four years ago. I wasn't watching anyone in particular, but I had felt a strange vibration in the web that I hadn't felt before, so naturally I followed it. I found myself in a dark parking lot, staring at a boy of fourteen crouched in a bush. He was hiding, waiting, and I attempted to speak to him, but he could not see me. I continued to wait and watch. Eventually, a pregnant woman came into view. She was fumbling with her keys, unaware of the boy's presence. Just as she reached her car, he scrambled from behind the bush. I saw the look of

desperation and fear in his eyes. I've seen it a hundred times before. He was lost. He was alone, and he was about to commit a desperate act on an unsuspecting woman.

"I drew the web within me in a way I didn't know was possible. I saw the vortex open before me as I moved between the woman and him. I'm not sure what followed, only that in the next instant we were in the watcher's realm. At first, I was relieved that I had saved the woman and the boy, but then I was overcome with fear. I had intervened. I had broken the one cardinal rule that should never be broken. I waited, watching the web for any ripples, any tears, but everything seemed to be intact. I convinced myself the vortex would have never opened for me if the boy had not been meant to alter. He would have carried out whatever it was he was planning without noticing me at all. It was almost as if the power of the web was inside me, fighting to preserve itself by preserving that woman. I watched Minnion closely just to be sure, and he adapted so well. He is gifted, truly gifted. As time went by, I saw no repercussions – until now." There was a sense of hopelessness in Gage's voice that tugged at Valeressa's own spot of emptiness that was never filled, no matter what she tried to shove into it. She pondered Minnion's relationship to Kaleb, and she wondered if there was a connection.

"Have you spoken to him about this? Have you talked about the circumstances surrounding his alteration?" she probed.

"No. Not a word. We've never spoken of it openly. It's more or less a shadow that follows us around."

"I'll speak to him," she finally agreed.

"And Valeressa," Gage reached out to touch her arm, and she felt a shudder. The man's face, which she had seen before, clouded her vision as if summoned by the touch. She stumbled backward, and Gage grabbed her hand to steady her.

"Valeressa? Are you okay? I didn't mean to catch you off guard," said a confused Gage. Valeressa laughed, and he was immediately at ease again.

"Oh, Gage. It's not you. I was just having one of my . . . moments." She tried to brush aside the unsettling feeling that was roosting in her chest, but it would not budge

even at the sound of her own confident reassurance. "Now, what were you about to say?"

"Oh," Gage's eyes shifted downward. "Please don't mention this to Master Burdock. He would not be pleased to hear that I bent the rules, even if I was trying to save a woman's life."

"You underestimate Master Burdock, Gage. He is very mindful of such things and very understanding when it comes to extraordinary circumstances. He trusts his watchers. He trusts you and your judgment. But yes, I will honor your request and not speak of this matter to him – for now. In the future, however –"

"Yes, I know," Gage interrupted. "It was a split-second decision. I felt compelled to act as if the web was demanding it. I couldn't stand by and watch him hurt her. She had the strongest attachments I've seen binding her to the web. The thought of those being severed was actually painful. I couldn't bear it."

"I think you made a wise decision, Gage, and I know Master Burdock would approve. Don't think of it anymore, and I'll see if I can do anything for Minnion."

***

She sought Minnion out at once, surprised to find him by himself though Gage had told her as much. He appeared to be distraught, which again was surprising for a watcher who had been among them for as long as he had.

"Hello there, Watcher Minnion," she addressed him as she approached. He did not look at her, nor did he respond to her greeting. She sat down beside him, but he scooted away from her.

"It might help if you talk to someone about whatever's bothering you. I'm told I'm a good listener," she prodded gently. He sat for quite some time without moving. She patiently waited, since she had nowhere else to be. She stretched her legs and shifted her position. He realized she wasn't going to leave him to himself as he wished.

"I'm fine. Now will you go away?" he snapped.

"Does my presence bother you for some reason?" she queried. His eyes shifted to meet her stare briefly, but he quickly averted them without answering.

"I know you know who I am," she said, puzzled by the change in his composure in response to her comment. "You brought Kaleb to see me, remember?" His tension eased ever so slightly at the mention of his friend's name.

"Yes, of course – Kaleb," his voice trailed off.

"Does this have something to do with Kaleb? I know you are the watcher who saved him. I know the circumstances surrounding his alteration. Are you second guessing yourself now? Has something happened between you two?" Valeressa knew that Kaleb had been grappling with his own doubts recently and may have distanced himself from Minnion as a result.

"No. No. Of course not. He'd be dead if it weren't for me. I would never regret saving a life," he retorted defensively. She had guessed wrong. If it wasn't Kaleb, then it must be something from his past life. That was usually the culprit, thus her next logical line of attack.

"Minnion, is it something from your past life?" she pressed. "I've found that memories do tend to creep up every once in a while. You certainly wouldn't be the first watcher to whom this has ever happened, and it really does help to talk about it."

"Your memories?" He kept his eyes fixed to the ground as he spoke in a tentative voice.

"No, not my memories. I'm referring to other watchers. I only tell you what has worked for them not what has worked from my own experience. I have no memories of my own." There was a hint of sadness in her voice.

"You don't remember anything from your other life?" She shook her head in response to his question. "I wish I couldn't remember, but I can't seem to forget."

"So, it is something from your past then?" He nodded a slow acknowledgment.

"Someone or something you saw while you were watching that triggered it, perhaps?" She attempted to fill in the unspoken gaps underlying his distress. He shrugged, and she scooted closer to him to pat him on the back. The pressure of her hand against him seemed to crumble his wall of silence.

"I hurt people," he admitted. She had heard this admission many times before in conversations with countless other watchers who lashed out at other people in an effort to ward off their own feelings of loneliness and isolation. "I'm ashamed of myself, so I try hard to help people – to redeem myself somehow. When I watch the web, I see how much I hurt people – people who were only trying to help me. I was only thinking of myself. I had so much anger bottled up inside of me, and I didn't know how to release it. If Gage hadn't –" his voice broke.

"Gage told me about what happened the night you altered."

"He did?"

"He did."

"What will happen to us now?"

"Whatever do you mean, Minnion? Nothing will happen to you. You know better than most that Master Burdock certainly would have wanted Gage to save the woman – and you. Besides, who said Master Burdock doesn't already know? He sees more than most, you know. Stop to think about it, Minnion. What would Kaleb have done without you? Not many watchers would have tried to save him, but you were his advocate, his only advocate. Even I doubted, but I'm glad I was wrong, and you were right. And there are countless others that you, and only you, could have saved and will be able to save in the future. Think forward not backward, Watcher Minnion. You have a gift."

He smiled slightly, but when he ventured another glance into her eyes, he quickly turned away again. She saw the shadow still clinging to him, unwilling to relinquish its hold in spite of her efforts.

"I'm curious about your name," she changed the subject to a lighter topic.

"Gage. He used to joke around with me that I was his underling – his minion. It sort of stuck. He was the first friend I have ever had – a true brother." She smiled.

"Do me a favor?" she asked. "Make peace with your past." She left him to ponder their conversation, hoping he would take her advice.

Valeressa walked back to stasis quickly. The entire time she had been waiting for

Minnion to talk, she was trying to push away the image of the man from her mind, but he would not go away. He came at the most inopportune times and fled just as suddenly. The longer she sat with Minnion, the clearer the image became until she had finally managed to drive it from the forefront of her mind. She was keenly aware that it hovered there still in her subconscious. She sat down, shaken by the experience. Kaleb's body lay there as it had for three long years, unmoving and statuesque. Sometimes she hated that it had to share this place with her, resented the intrusion in her private, personal space, and yet she knew she should not feel that way. It was not the watcher's way.

She thought about what she had told Minnion, about his despair over his past life. She came to the realization that the face that was stalking her mind was most likely a memory from her own past life trying to break free from its imprisonment. She did not know how to release it any more than she knew how to make herself fit in with the other watchers. She felt drawn to the other realm, a realm she could not enter. She felt a sadness hang a blind over her heart, blocking her sense of belonging and contentment. She suddenly felt very tired and had the urge to sleep, though she knew watchers did not need to sleep any more than they needed to eat. She did not try, however, to fight the fatigue that meandered through her. Instead, she surrendered to it, her mind grabbing wildly for the image of the man before numbing itself with a kind of wakeful slumber.

Chapter 5: am i

am i

i'm tired but I cannot sleep

the dark surrounds me and seeps inside

i'm tainted by the devil's touch

i'm branded by the flames of hell's torment

i'm sinking in the tar pits of life

my soul screams in fear but its voice is silent

the wind blows in my ear but there is no breeze

i feel the heat but the sun does not shine

and the dark engulfs me in its lonely caress

i cry tears of confusion but my cheeks are dry

i see raindrops falling from an invisible sky

i hear a voice but see no man

i see swords clashing, guns firing, but i see no war

i see pen and paper but there is no writing

i see a face but no smile for its lips do not exist

i smell a rose but see no petals

i see a hand but cannot grasp

i'm wide awake yet fast asleep

i see the darkness thicken and become one with me

i am touching the ground but i'm suspended in air
lightning flashes but its light is black
my eyes are searching but find nothing
i am here and yet do not live
i breathe and yet I get no air
i'm drowning but there is no water
i'm tired but I cannot sleep
the dark surrounds me and seeps inside...

~ Jessie Watson

Jessie had never felt so isolated before. She had once again seen a fragile glimmer of hope, and she had to watch as she crushed it with her very own hand. She couldn't force herself to go to school again, nor could she make herself talk to Shane again. She could never fit in anywhere. Somehow, she had always known that. Her life was like a slow-moving, silent film with vague images and nonexistent dialogue. The plot was never emerging, and the drudgery was filmed in black and white: gray tones for a gray life. The realm in which Kaleb lived seemed so much more desirable, which was probably why she believed everything he had told her about the watchers and their web.

Jessie kept her blinds closed all night, not feeling the slightest urge to peek out to see what Shane was up to. While she couldn't quite put her finger on the reason behind the sudden shift in her mood, she couldn't escape it either. One moment of awkward conversation had pushed her over the precipice of validation upon which she had been teetering.

The next morning, she told Mrs. Moore that she wasn't feeling well and couldn't go to school. She stayed in her room all day long, not bothering to shower or change her clothes. She felt no better by nightfall, although Mrs. Moore convinced her to eat a little something for dinner. When the sun shone again through the cracks in her blinds announcing the dawning of a new day, she smothered it by putting her pillow over her head. Mrs. Moore knocked on the door to see if she was feeling any better, opening it a crack when she got no response. Seeing Jessie bundled under the blankets on her bed, Mrs. Moore decided that she must still be under the weather. She tiptoed into the room, leaving a glass of orange juice and a bagel on her night stand.

As soon as Mrs. Moore was gone, Jessie uncovered her head. She couldn't go on like this forever. She took a sip of the juice and nibbled on the bagel, deep in thought. Before that morning, she hadn't felt as though altering was her decision, but now she knew that if she truly wanted to alter, she could. If she felt hopeless before, it was nothing compared to what she felt now.

Jessie could actually feel the darkness slither toward her, ready to snuff out her existence. Was this how Kaleb had felt? As her mind drifted to thoughts of Kaleb, she wondered where he was now. Was he watching with anticipation so his wait could be over – so he could move on? She wished she could talk to him, but he had left her all alone – some watcher he was. The darkness of her thoughts continued to engulf her like a thick vapor, trying to suffocate her.

She found it difficult to breathe. Her hands trembled. She sat on her bed as if in a trance. Hours passed, and she didn't move an inch. She was being asphyxiated by her despair, and she felt resistance was useless. When she could no longer see the rays of the sun trying to sneak through her blinds, she knew they had finally given way to the shadows of the night. She began to cry, but only for a moment.

Surprised that altering had somehow eluded her, Jessie realized she had to snap out of her current state of catatonia. She needed some fresh air, and she knew from the silence of the house that no one was home. After taking a quick shower to clear her head, she settled into a cushioned chair outside on the deck for a change of scenery – darkness still, but nonetheless, a change. She was absorbed in feeling the cool night breeze with her eyes closed when she heard his voice.

"So, what's up with you? Skipping school?" Shane was talking to her through the fence. She supposed she couldn't avoid him forever, now that watcher's realm seemed to be closed to her.

"Just not feeling well the last couple of days," her voice was barely audible. She hadn't spoken in nearly two days, so her voice was hoarse.

"I figured as much when you didn't open your blinds. I hope I didn't do anything to offend you?" his voice raised on the last word, forming the sentence into a question rather than the statement he had intended.

"Nah. It's all me. Believe at least that much," she muttered.

"Do you want to talk about it?" he inquired.

"I seriously doubt you'd want to hear it," she responded blankly. With that, Shane jumped over the fence with a little too much ease. He'd clearly had practice with this sort of thing before, probably on one of his late-night crusades with his friends.

"Try me," he urged with a smile. He sat on the grass by the edge of the deck with his legs crossed.

"What do you want to know?"

"Well, why did you ditch us so fast the other day when we walked you home?"

"It's complicated," she stated simply, trying to dodge the question.

"It's not that complicated, Jessie. I'm thinking you don't care much for my friends, particularly Nikki," he speculated.

She looked away, but responded, "Shane, you have been so nice to me over the last week or so. You're the first person who has noticed me since I came to this school, but I don't fit in with you or your friends. I'm a nobody. No friends. No family. You wouldn't understand." Her voice cracked as she finished, giving way to the raw emotion that now swept over her.

"You're right, you know," his voice filled the silence with deafening clarity. "I don't understand anything about you or your life. I was just trying to be nice, but no one will ever understand you if you keep pushing them away."

"Why do you care anyway?" she asked angrily.

"I've never seen anyone look as sad as you did the day we met. No one deserves to feel like that. I want to be your friend, to see if I can make you smile," he explained. She thought back to the day they ran into each other. She remembered her encounter with Kaleb, and the conclusions she'd drawn about his relationship with her.

"Kaleb," the word escaped her lips before she could stop herself. She hadn't meant to say his name out loud. How could she explain Kaleb to him? Her mind wandered again, unaware that Shane was staring at her with a puzzled expression on his face. Where was Kaleb? Why hadn't she seen him tonight?

"Kaleb who?" Shane's curiosity piqued.

"Oh, you wouldn't know him. His name was Kaleb Scott," she spoke the words without thinking.

"Kaleb Scott!" Shane's reaction certainly wasn't what she had expected.

"Do you know him?" she asked, the realization of the trouble she may have just brewed settling over her like a strait jacket.

"Well, I did once," he replied, "but how do you know him?"

"That's a long story. How do you know him?" she countered, trying to deflect any further investigation on his part.

"Well, if it's the same Kaleb Scott, his dad was my dad's boss, and our families spent a lot of time together. I was good friends with Kaleb, even though he was a few years older than me. He was almost like my big brother…" Shane didn't finish the thought, his countenance changing from curiosity to sadness.

"What happened?" she asked, although she already knew Kaleb's side of the story. She couldn't believe that Shane actually knew him. She knew Kaleb had lived in this same town, but to be so tightly connected with Shane, like a brother? How does a bond like that get broken? She needed to hear the tale from a different perspective.

"First, let me ask you a question. Have you seen him lately?" His eyes were wild with anticipation, but Jessie knew she couldn't tell him the truth about Kaleb. She would have to lie and hope that Shane believed her.

"No, I haven't. Not for a long time. I had just been remembering him that day I plowed into you," she answered, looking away so he wouldn't see the deception in her eyes. She was thankful that she had the cover of darkness to mask her expression, since it seemed easier to tell lies when her face blended into with the shadows.

"Oh," he responded somberly, taking a deep breath before continuing. "Kaleb's parents died in a tragic car accident. He took it pretty hard. Who wouldn't, especially when you think your uncle was responsible for it all?" It was Jessie's turn to be surprised. Kaleb said he had no family. She continued to listen intently now.

"After his parents died, he lost his will to live, I think. He wouldn't talk to anyone. He completely isolated himself. He was angry and so full of hate. I tried to call him. My dad tried to reach out to him. He wouldn't listen to anyone. Even though the police report indicated the crash was an unfortunate accident, he still blamed his Uncle Bradley, who had been driving the car. Bradley apparently hit some black ice on the road, careening into oncoming traffic and rolling the car several times, but Kaleb was convinced he had been drunk. Bradley almost died too. He was in a medically induced coma for a while, so he couldn't talk to Kaleb about it."

"I didn't know he had an uncle," Jessie admitted.

"Bradley wasn't actually Kaleb's blood relative. Kaleb's dad, Wade, met Bradley when he was participating in a big brother program. Bradley's parents weren't in the picture, and he had picked up some pretty bad habits.

Wade took him under his wing and helped him straighten out his life. Wade convinced his parents to adopt Bradley, which they did. Unfortunately, Bradley had a relapse when Kaleb was a kid. He drove home drunk one night and hit someone. Luckily, the victim wasn't seriously injured, but Bradley did some jail time over it. He went through AA and really turned his life around, but Kaleb couldn't forgive him. When Kaleb found out Bradley had been behind the wheel when his parents died, he went berserk. Kaleb was sure his uncle had been drinking, even though Bradley had been sober for a while. That's when Kaleb withdrew." Shane shrugged his shoulders and shook his head with disappointment.

"What happened to Kaleb?" Jessie asked.

"I don't know. I guess he went away somewhere to start over. He asked my dad to manage his parents' estate for him, but my dad hasn't heard from him in three years. No one has," he turned to look curiously at Jessie again, "until you came along, that is."

"I haven't seen Kaleb in a long time like I told you, certainly not in the last three years," she quickly replied, and then added, "it must have been before all of this happened. Maybe we aren't thinking of the same person at all." Shane didn't look convinced, but he didn't press her for any more information. What she couldn't get out of her mind was the fact that Kaleb willed himself to be forgotten. He willingly broke all of his bonds, in some cases, hurting those who cared about him, like Shane and his uncle. Why had he left all of that out of his story?

"Do you still see Bradley around?" Jessie asked Shane.

"No, I had only seen him a few times before the accident when I was with Kaleb. Why do you ask?"

"Just curious," Jessie said. She was glad that Shane jumped over the fence tonight. The darkness that seemed to be extracting her very being had been dispelled by his presence. She felt better, and she realized that she could move forward with her life now that she knew Shane was her friend. She also felt an urgent need to see Kaleb. He couldn't disappear now, when his memory was so clear to those who knew him. He couldn't be invisible forever if they were waiting for him to return. Could he?

Interlude 3

Valeressa felt consciousness nudging her back from wherever she had gone – somewhere she could not remember now. The face had been there with her, trying to pull her along with him. She was scared and resolved to go directly to Master Burdock. He was not hard to find, and he had likely already sensed her coming before she ever arrived.

"Valeressa! And how are you today?" He had seen the grave expression on her face, but asked the question anyway.

"Master Burdock, something most peculiar has happened, and I seek your council." She launched into an explanation as he watched, his face not revealing the slightest bit of intrigue – almost as if he had been expecting such a tale.

"Most interesting. Most interesting indeed," he said as he stroked his white goatee.

"But what does it mean?" she queried.

"That I do not know for certain, but I believe you have surmised correctly in thinking that your past has finally found you."

"But what do I do Master Burdock?"

"That I must leave to your wisdom," he said. She twirled a long red lock of her hair in frustration. She knew he would say no more concerning the matter.

"And what of Kaleb?" he asked as she turned to leave. Of course, he would inquire about his pet project. Why concern himself with such a minor event compared to the one she had just experienced?

"No change," she answered curtly before excusing herself. As she walked along the path to her dwelling in agitation, she saw a figure standing by her door, waiting for her return. She was hardly in the mood for idle chit-chat with a watcher at the moment. As she came closer, she recognized the face.

"Hello, Kaleb," she said flatly, still angry about her encounter with Master Burdock.

"Is this a bad time? You don't seem quite yourself," Kaleb asked, though she could see the longing in his eyes. He needed to talk, and she had been entrusted with his care. She set aside her frustration, which was a perk of being in the watcher's realm. She found that she could maneuver her feelings around, bringing one to the forefront while sending another to a point outside of her focus. The feelings didn't go away, but she could deal with them at a later time, most likely while she was in stasis where she could see more clearly.

"No, not at all. I told you to come to me anytime you needed to talk, didn't I? I think this qualifies as anytime," she smiled reassuringly as she spoke.

"You remember that girl I told you about. Jessie?" Valeressa nodded her head, and he continued, "Well, I don't think I can watch her anymore. I've been spending too much time with her, and now she's formed an attachment with a strand I can't see. I can't see her clearly anymore. My emotions are clouding my view. I feel like the web is swallowing me, and I can't stand outside it anymore like I'm supposed too. I'm confused. I don't know what to do?"

"Why are you afraid to follow your heart, Kaleb?"

"My heart? My heart? How can you talk to me about my heart? You don't know anything about me or my heart," he looked away from her for a moment to regain his composure. She watched him closely.

"I'm sorry," he finally said. "I didn't mean to lash out at you like that. It's just that I can't – I can't open my heart. It would be like opening a coffin, and desecrating those feelings I've so carefully buried there. I would have to dredge through all of the pain again because I'm afraid this realm hasn't healed me completely. It only allowed me to bury my pain, and it's a fairly shallow grave at that. I don't bear anymore hostility toward my uncle, and for that I am grateful. The web taught me how to overcome those feelings, but not the sadness, not the grief. I can't open my heart. It's all I have left. Besides, I could never be good enough for someone like her. She deserves better – she

deserves more."

"Kaleb, you need to let Jessie make her own decisions about what is best for her. And you need to realize that you can't hide forever. At some point your grave will be unearthed. You know that, don't you? Deep down, you know you'll have to let go of those feelings. Why not now? Why not surrender to the web, and see what happens? You might be surprised by what you find."

"That's not my purpose –"

"How do you know?" He looked at her quizzically as if she had broken her vow of protection by suggesting such a thing.

"But I made my choice that night when Minnion came for me. I made my choice!"

"Did you?" she continued to probe, willing him to understand.

"Yes, I did. I chose to leave just like I'm leaving now," he got up and walked briskly away. Valeressa watched him sadly, hoping he would ponder what she had said to him and try to dig under the double meanings she had hinted at before doing anything brash.

Chapter 6: Just Tell Me Why

Just Tell Me Why

You're nowhere at all,
When I stumble and fall.
You're nowhere at all,
When I need someone to call.
And you're nowhere to be found,
When I'm startled by a sound.
You're not there,
When life isn't fair.
You're not there,
To be impressed by the clothes I wear.
You're not there,
So I don't care.
And I don't know why,
You're making me cry.
And I don't know why,
You've made love a lie.
But my biggest fear,
Is that you'll never be here
And I know it's true,

That I don't know you.
And maybe it's fate,
That you're running late.
Or maybe love's not meant for me,
And I'm too blind to see -
That you only exist,
In my dreams when I'm kissed.
And you pass by in my mind at night,
And no matter if I try with all my might -
You'll never be real for me to touch.
And maybe I know at least that much.
So why is a tear falling from my eye?
And why can't I let you go and say goodbye?
Why can't I accept the reality before me,
Instead of attempting to flee?
Just tell me why,
I should continue to try.
Just tell me why,
I have to be so darn shy.
Just tell me why,
The sun still has to rise in the sky.
Just tell me why,
I can't just die.

~ Jessie Watson

Jessie managed to make it through school the next day without incident. Shane was overly friendly, and honestly, Nikki didn't seem to mind. Jessie wondered what he had said about her to Nikki. She was relieved that Shane seemed to have gone somewhere with his friends right after school, so she wouldn't have to walk home trying to avoid him and his "pack." Her eyes shifted eagerly toward the tree as she drew near. She wasn't sure exactly what she'd say to Kaleb if she saw him. Should she tell him what she knew about him? How would he react? Did he know what had nearly happened to her last night?

Her heart raced as she recognized his familiar form coming more clearly into view with each step she took. This time he joined her instead of waiting for her at the tree. Although she'd done it many times before, for the first time, Jessie felt strange walking next to him on the sidewalk in broad daylight, fully aware that no one else could see him.

"Jessie, we need to talk. Would you mind too much if we went to my property?" Kaleb's voice was somber, and Jessie's heart sank.

"Sure. Let me tell Mrs. Moore that I have to go to the library." He was silent the rest of the way to the Moore's house, as well as on the bus ride to the property. He didn't speak until they reached the top of the hill that overlooked the barn. He sat down next to a tree on the path, and she followed his lead.

"So…" he looked uncomfortable. Jessie couldn't take the suspense any longer.

"Is this about last night?" she asked, but he shook his head no.

"Do you know what happened to me last night?" she queried further. Again, he shook his head no. How could that be? She was sure that she had been about to alter.

"Where were you?" she continued, trying to draw him out of his muted contemplation.

"Jessie…" he paused, "I can't do this anymore."

"What do you mean, Kaleb? I thought this 'watching business' was what you were supposed to do!" Her mind was flooded once again with her fears that he was tired of being around her. He was tired of trying to pretend to be interested in what happened to her. She looked at him for reassurance, but he was staring off into the distance.

"Kaleb, I thought I was about to alter last night. I felt this darkness sucking the life out of me. I waited for you, but you never came. I was alone. I was scared. I went outside to find you, and Shane happened to see me." Kaleb seemed shocked by her words, as if he had no idea what to think. Jessie continued, "He saved me, Kaleb. If Shane hadn't come along, I'm not sure what I would have done, but you can imagine my surprise that he knows who you are." Kaleb looked away again in utter disbelief, still unable to speak.

Mistakenly thinking Kaleb was angry, Jessie quickly explained, "I didn't mean to mention your name. I was thinking it, but I didn't realize I was thinking out loud. Shane heard it and that led to our conversation about you. You can imagine how different his story was from the one you told me. Kaleb, you lied to me. You told me you had no one – that you'd been forgotten, but you have an uncle who cares about you, and Shane thinks of you as his brother. How can you tell me that you understand anything about me or my life when you had people who cared about you, and you threw it away?" Her hands were shaking – she had never spoken so angrily with anyone before. She thought she might faint as her heart pounded harder and harder. Kaleb turned to face her.

"Kaleb, there is no such thing as no strings attached with you. You cut your strings and severed the bonds of your own free will." Finally, he spoke.

"Jessie. This isn't about me. I perhaps reacted harshly when my world went topsy-turvy. I admit that. While I see the world differently now, what's done is done. There's no turning back. There's nothing I can do about it now. I would have hoped that you of all people, knowing me as well as you do in such a short time, could understand why I reacted as I did, but I guess you've never known what it is like to be loved by parents. I relied on them for everything – love, advice, encouragement, praise, comfort, hope. I was who I was only because of them. When they died, I died too."

Jessie felt the sting of his words, though he hadn't meant to hurt her feelings. She had always been jealous of anyone who had loving parents, but he didn't have to rub it in her face. His words only widened the ever-growing crevasse between them, solidifying the fact that in the mortal world their paths would have never crossed. She tried to choke back her tears unsuccessfully. He turned to look at her again, and his eyes filled with sadness as he watched a tear fall silently down her cheek. It seemed to remind him of the reason he had asked to talk to her in the first place.

"Jessie, my purpose now is to find forgotten souls and offer them the opportunity to alter into the watcher's realm. Usually, I know only a short time before they are ready to alter, and they can only see me a short while before the altering occurs. Unfortunately for me, that didn't happen with you. Jessie, I've been watching you for two and a half years. I've gotten to know more about you than almost any other person I've known in my entire life. I've spent too much time with you, gotten too close to you…" He seemed to want to say more, but he stopped short.

Was he trying to tell her that he loved her? She had a hard time believing that thought because she felt more like he was trying to let her down slowly. Had he sensed that she had fallen in love with him, but didn't reciprocate the feeling?

"Jessie, I'm glad you met Shane. He really is a great guy, and he may make this easier for you."

"What?" she could not believe this. Her tone was more than agitated now, "You think I like Shane? Look, Kaleb, Shane and I are barely friends. I've only known him for two weeks, and our longest conversation was about you for crying out loud. I admit, I was infatuated with the guy for a while, but that was before I met you, before I –"

"Jessie," Kaleb cut her off before she could tell him that it was before she knew what love was, which would have sounded ridiculous since Kaleb wasn't real in the mortal sense of the word.

"I have to go. I'm leaving. I can't do my work as a watcher with you. I can't see your strand clearly because I'm too involved. I didn't have an inkling that you might be close to altering last night, or I would have been there. And I think I finally figured out why I never knew that you and Shane were becoming friends. You bonded with the same person with whom I severed a bond. Because I broke that bond with Shane, I'm not allowed to see it, even as a watcher. Most people who are watchers have left no one behind, but I'm the exception to the rule. I'm leaving for your own good. I hope you understand, Jessie. I didn't realize what was happening between us before it was too late. I'm sorry. I'm so sorry."

She had been staring at the barn, trying to make sense of what he was telling her. She wanted to scream at him to stop, but she could not form the words. She turned to look at him as he finished his last apology, hoping to think of some way to convince him not to leave, but he was already gone. She was alone, again. Fresh tears streamed down her face, and she laughed as she said aloud, "Jessie, you are a stupid, stupid girl. Your imaginary friends won't even stick around."

She didn't remember how or when she made it home. The afternoon was a blur of disbelief. She had seen this coming. She'd had her joy ride, but now her train of pleasure had been derailed. Yet, her only regret was not seeing Kaleb's face one last time, not seeing his tousled blonde hair, his piercing blue eyes, or his boyish grin. *Just tell me why*, she thought to herself numbly. If only she could have said goodbye. If only he would have said goodbye. Why was he apologizing for giving her the best few months of her life? She had lost hope, but he had given it back to her. He had become her one true friend – the only person to have known her and actually stuck around, until now. She was sorry that their last conversation had been riddled with accusations, anger, and tension. *If only*, she thought, but she stopped herself because she knew that if onlys would never bring him back. *Just tell me why*, she thought again, but there was no one to answer.

***

Shane caught up to her after school the next day. Much to her relief, he was alone. "Hey, do you want to go to a movie with us this weekend?" he asked.

"No thanks, Shane. I would make an idiot of myself in front of your friends," she replied dryly.

"Well, how about with just me then?" he persisted.

"Yeah, I'm sure Nikki would love that!" Jessie said sarcastically.

"Nikki would be fine with that. She knows how it is with us," he reassured her.

She stopped walking to ask, "And exactly how is it with us?"

"Well, we're friends. Besides, you're the first person I've met in the last three years who knew Kaleb. Listen, Jessie, it's nice to be around someone who knew him."

"Oh, so this is all about Kaleb then?" she said defensively. Hearing his name made her feel empty inside. Why was everything in her life tied to him?

"Jessie, you can be so difficult sometimes. We're friends, okay?"

"Okay," she sighed.

"I miss him too, you know. Boy, he sure had one sweet ride!"

"Yeah, tell me about it," she agreed as she remembered sitting behind the wheel, smelling the leather interior. She stopped the memory before she got to the part about the person she was with, his eyes, his smile, his hair, his kindness, his laugh…

"Wait! You knew Kaleb when he graduated?" he asked. Jessie had said too much, again. How could she backtrack? She realized she couldn't, so she'd have to roll with it.

"Yeah," she replied quietly, hoping he would drop it.

"It's odd that he never mentioned you to me or me to you, don't you think?" he inquired. She shrugged nonchalantly while panic crept over her.

"Not really. Why would he mention someone like me? It's not like I was anything but an acquaintance at that. We didn't really walk in the same social circles. Besides, I only know about the truck because I saw him driving it around after graduation. I certainly didn't know him as well as you did." Jessie's astuteness in concocting lies on the spot surprised herself. Shane seemed to be mulling over her story, and she knew he wasn't going to let her off the hook. His scrutinizing eyes were staring her down, trying to extract information and emotions she didn't want to reveal.

"If you didn't know him well, then why would you be crying over him three years after he left?" Shane questioned, referring to the time she had run into him.

"I guess I liked him a lot more than he liked me, and I never got over it. Now will you drop it?" she snipped. Jessie's irate tone caught Shane off guard.

"Oh, I get it," he was obviously embarrassed that he had pried.

"I'm really trying to forget about it, and you're not helping," she clarified.

"I guess that makes us an odd pairing then, doesn't it? You're trying to forget him, and I'm trying to remember him," he tried to chuckle at the thought. She gave him a half smile.

"So…about the movie?" Shane wasn't going to give up. Jessie welcomed the thought of a pleasant distraction with her new found friend.

"Okay. Okay. I'll go if you'll quit bugging me about it," she relented. Shane noticed the obvious change in her demeanor; she actually looked happy for the first time since he'd met her.

Friday finally arrived. Mrs. Moore was seemed surprised but pleased when Jessie told her she was going out that weekend. She nearly quit breathing for a full minute when Jessie told her she was going to the movie with Shane Gunderson, and she was uncommonly speechless when Shane actually appeared at the door, as if she thought Jessie had been lying to her.

"I think you might have given Mrs. Moore a heart condition," Jessie joked as Shane opened her door. She was surprised at how easily the conversation flowed as they talked mostly about school. The movie was a fantasy/thriller, which Jessie really enjoyed. For two hours, she was so completely engrossed in the movie that her mind never wandered toward her own life, providing the escape she needed. Shane was such a gentleman as well, opening the doors for her and insisting on paying for her ticket. She remembered how often he had filled her dreams – how often she had actually dreamed of this moment with him. That memory made her feel like a wolf in sheep's clothing, but things were so different now. She had come under the premise of friendship, nothing more. Her silly infatuation of the past was all but forgotten. The blue eyes that haunted her dreams at night now belonged to a mirage – a mere illusion that would never materialize into reality no matter how hard she wished.

"So, what does the future hold for you, Jessie Watson?" Shane asked as he drove his dad's car out of the theater parking lot.

"Well, that's a tough one. When a ward of the state like me graduates from high school, the government calls it emancipation, but I feel more like I'm walking the plank. I'm not sure what will get me first, the water or the sharks," she answered truthfully.

"That was a dumb question to ask. I'm sorry, Jessie, I forgot…" He didn't finish his sentence, but he instinctively reached his hand over to touch hers in an effort to ease the discomfort he had caused. She couldn't push away the flutters in her stomach, but she resisted the urge to smile with all her might. She looked out the window at the passing cars, and he withdrew his hand as casually as he had placed it on hers. She tried to imagine if that's how Kaleb's hand would have felt the day he reached for hers in front of the barn. When she had thought of holding Kaleb's hand, she couldn't imagine what it would feel like because she had never felt the touch of a boy's skin on her own. She didn't have any trouble imagining it now.

"Thanks for the movie, Shane. I mean that. Thanks for insisting that I come," she said, finally releasing her smile from its imprisonment.

"Do you know this was the first time I've been to a movie theater in years?" she asked, lightening the uneasiness that was still present.

"You're kidding me! You've got to get out more, Jessie!" He was astonished, and that led the way for a more light-hearted conversation before he rounded the corner to the Moore's driveway. He opened the car door and escorted her to the front porch. There was no awkwardness between them, no anticipation of a hug or a kiss, just a general gratitude for the friendship they shared and for the bond they shared with Kaleb. Jessie, too, liked to be around someone who had known Kaleb when he was alive.

Kaleb had altered her life, although not in the way he intended. She only wished they had met under different circumstances - normal rather than paranormal. Jessie learned from her reading novels that even in times of hopelessness, love endured and became stronger because of the obstacles. She may never know the answer to the why, but she could hold onto her hope and her memory of her first love. After all, his image was still permanently etched in her mind. Her strand was entwined with his so intricately that they could never be separated. Jessie had fallen in love with him, and she was sure that he had developed feelings for her as well.

Interlude 4

"Master Burdock?"

"Yes, Valeressa. What is it?" Master Burdock seemed distracted.

"It's Kaleb," she said. He focused his attention on her now, raising his eyebrows questioningly. "He's refusing to watch the girl anymore. He says she's formed an attachment with someone whose strand he cannot see."

"This is true," Master Burdock affirmed.

"But Master Burdock, he told her he was not going to watch her anymore. He severed the connection between the two of them," her voice was pleading for guidance.

"Valeressa, he has saved the girl. She will stay in the other realm."

"But what of Kaleb?"

"It appears he has made his choice."

"But did he know he had a choice? He thinks he made the choice the night he altered. He doesn't know he can go back. I've said nothing to him of his body being kept in stasis. If he knew he could return . . . I tried to guide him. I told him to follow his heart, but I don't think he understood."

"Valeressa, my child. You have done all you can do. The choice has always been his to make. He senses that, and he has made his choice. He continues to pull against the web of his own accord. No one forces him to hold his heart closed. No one forces him to stay."

"But he only chose to stay here because he believes the girl deserves someone better than him. He still clings to his past; thus, the choice cannot have been made or he would have drawn on the web to fill the holes in his heart."

"Very perceptive, Valeressa. Very perceptive. Remember the options. One – he

stays in the watcher's realm. Two – he returns to the other realm. Three – he continues to cling to both realms, unable to make a choice, thus resulting in his extinction. It does appear that he is heading in the direction of extinction, does it not? He thinks he has chosen, but his heart is still in limbo." Master Burdock discussed Kaleb's apparently inevitable extinction with too much serenity.

"Something must be done. We cannot allow that to happen!"

"I cannot override his will, no matter what you wish, no matter what I wish. It would destroy our connection to the web. It would destroy all of us."

"So, nothing can be done?" Her voice was dripping with desperation.

"Not by us. Not by us. His fate lies in the girl's hands now. We shall see if she can find a way to save him as he has saved her."

"Watch and wait," she whispered.

"That's what we do, is it not?" She dismissed herself, feeling agitated again. She wished she could draw on the power of the web to mollify her rising fear, her dread of what was to come. Watch and wait. Watch and wait indeed! She felt herself strain against the pull of the web. She would not intervene, however, for she did not want to disrupt the sanctity of the web that held them all together. She would not seek Kaleb out, instead she withdrew. She entered stasis and waited for the image to return to her mind so she could rest in its gaze.

Chapter 7: Hope

How?

How does the bird sing when winter snow flies?
How does the chick hatch when the shell won't break?
How does the moon still shine on a clouded night?
And how can a smile come from a sick child's face?

How can there be so much pain and hatred on an earth
created with love?
How can the human race survive with all of the drugs?
How can a fish exist in a frozen lake?
And how can a bear live with a rifleman's bullet?

How can one doubt the love of another?
How can a fight result in the loss of a brother?
Hope is the answer to the how,
And how is the question to the hope!

~ Jessie Watson

Jessie had been going to Kaleb's land on the weekends. She sat on the top of the hill and stared into the forest. How could such beauty be accompanied by so much sadness? This was her third visit. She always had a secret wish that she would see Kaleb there. She could so clearly picture his face in her head.

She was so absorbed in her thoughts that she was startled to hear a twig snap in the path behind her. She was frozen with fear. She had been so shortsighted to come to a secluded wood all by herself. She tried to push from her mind the images of her dead body lying beneath a thicket, obscured from view. Kaleb had once told her no one ever came here, but then again, she had the impression that he hadn't visited the place very often himself. Her heart was pounding hard as the adrenaline coursed through her veins.

"This is private property," boomed the sound of the deep male voice behind her. She turned her head slowly to face her fear. She didn't dare look up to see his face; she wasn't ready to meet her fate.

She kept her eyes cast down and simply stammered, "I…I…I…didn't mean any harm. I'll leave." She stepped to the side of the path in an effort to go around him, but the stranger moved directly in front of her, blocking her only escape. She continued looking down, frantically trying to think of a way out of this mess, but no alternative ended well for her.

"What are you doing here?" the voice demanded. Apparently, he was not going to give up without some answers. Her hands were trembling. Was this the end she had chosen for herself? Would mourning the loss of Kaleb be her own demise?

"I come here to think sometimes. It's peaceful." The explanation was weak, and the words sounded lame even as she heard herself utter them. Would that be enough for him to let her pass?

No, the interrogation continued, "How did you find this place?" She hesitated, probably too long. He would think she was trying to fabricate a lie, which she was, but how much of the truth could she disclose without being institutionalized? She had no idea who this man was. Should she tell him part of the truth, mentioning Kaleb's name? She couldn't see any way around it. She certainly would have never ventured out here on her own without a guide. She decided she had no choice.

"Kaleb Scott brought me here once," she mumbled softly.

"Kaleb?" he said, evidently startled by the mention of the name. The way the man said Kaleb's name made it sound as if he was asking her a question, and his silence insisted that she say more. What did he want to know? She couldn't tell him much more. She managed to force her gaze from the ground, trying to assess his reaction from his facial expression. She was taken back by what she saw. This man looked oddly familiar, but she couldn't place where she had seen him before. She was trying to reassure herself that it wasn't on an FBI Most Wanted poster.

When she didn't willingly offer any information, he probed further, "Have you seen Kaleb lately?"

"No, not for a long time," she responded truthfully, but he glared at her skeptically.

"Who are you?" His face shaded with distrust as his eyes narrowed.

"My name is Jessie. I was a friend of Kaleb's," she quickly replied, trying desperately to ease his concern and unprovoked hostility.

"I don't remember a Jessie," he muttered to himself, his brow knit in concentration as if his mind was clicking through images of Kaleb's friends. She surmised that he was someone who had known Kaleb well – someone who was looking out for the property until Kaleb returned. Maybe Shane's father? No, the face didn't match, and he had black hair. This man's hair was more the color of Jessie's own hair, and he sported a neatly trimmed goatee.

"I met Kaleb after his parents' accident," she offered, hoping he would drop his line of questioning and let her go.

"Oh," he said under his breath, as if he didn't want to dredge up any pain. Then his eyes shifted, doubtful of her explanation. "I thought Kaleb withdrew from his friends after the accident?" Again, his statement sounded more like a question, and he was waiting rather impatiently for her answer. She was still trying to figure out his connection to Kaleb. His last comment made it sound as though he hadn't seen Kaleb since the accident and was relying on third party observations rather than his own personal interaction. She decided her best way out of this inquisition was diversion.

"You never mentioned your name. How do you know Kaleb?" she asked nervously. The question caught him off guard.

"I'm Bradley Scott, Kaleb's uncle," he continued eyeing her suspiciously as he spoke, but everything made sense now. Jessie had finally come face to face with the elusive uncle who, unbeknownst to him, was partially responsible for her meeting Kaleb in the first place.

Bradley was still talking, so Jessie tuned back in, "I've been keeping an eye on the place. A while back, someone thought they saw a vehicle driving erratically out here." She tried to control her emotions as she digested the fact that someone had witnessed her driving lesson the night Kaleb had first shown her his property! She tried to assure herself that no one could have seen her face. Again, she attempted to change the topic of conversation back to him.

"Kaleb's uncle? I've heard of you. It's a pleasure to finally make your acquaintance," she exaggerated, trying to sound casual and pleasant, although she was still on red alert, trying to find a way out of her predicament.

"Kaleb mentioned me to you?"

"No," she admitted, and quickly added, "Shane Gunderson told me about you." His hazel eyes were wide with shock, but she knew very well that Kaleb had pretty much ceased to acknowledge his uncle's existence after the accident.

"You know Shane Gunderson? It looks like you've got the advantage on me."

"Shane is my neighbor."

"I see. Has Shane mentioned seeing Kaleb recently?"

"Neither of us have seen in a couple of years at least."

"That's not news to me. He pretty much disappeared." The tension in his face was replaced by sadness and regret. He relaxed his muscular stance, and Jessie knew her interrogation was drawing to a close.

"Yeah," Jessie agreed, "you can say that again." *Literally*, she thought. Jessie broke the uncomfortable silence, "Well, I better be heading back. It's getting late."

"Can I give you a ride?" he offered unexpectedly. Jessie's face must have shown her alarm. She didn't know him after all; she merely knew of him. Since the last time Shane saw him, he certainly could have turned into a crazed lunatic, and he did have a jail record. She was letting her imagination get away from her again. Though she knew her fears were probably unwarranted, she was still hesitant to accept a ride from this stranger. Bradley must have sensed her concern when she didn't immediately answer him.

"Your mom probably taught you not to accept rides from strangers," he speculated.

"I don't have a mom," she retorted. She hadn't meant to reveal that fact, but it always struck a nerve when someone assumed that she had a mom who actually cared enough about her to give her any caution at all. His eyebrow rose, questioning her curt response.

"Oh, I'm sorry to hear that," he sympathized in a tone reserved for someone mourning the loss of a close relative.

"She didn't die," Jessie corrected him. "At least I don't think she died. I never knew who she was. She kind of abandoned me to pursue other interests."

"I'm sorry to hear that too. Look. I promise I'm not going to hurt you, but if there really is someone prowling around out here, besides you, I would feel better if you let me take you home," his deep voice sounded concerned and kind, although a shiver ran down her spine at the thought of someone prowling around in the woods. She had let her guard down coming out here alone. She assumed that Kaleb was still secretly watching out for her, but what could he have done if someone tried to hurt her? She shuttered at that thought, vowing never to return.

"Okay," she conceded. He kept his distance as he escorted her to his black Dodge Ram truck. She climbed in, and he started the engine.

"You say you live by Shane Gunderson then?" he asked as if he had just trapped her in a lie. She thought they were past all the conjecture now, but he still didn't believe her.

"Yes, he lives in the house behind the Moore's. Those are my foster parents," she reassured him.

"How long have you been in foster care, if you don't mind me asking?"

"As long as I can remember," she answered matter-of-factly, although she did mind him asking personal questions. She supposed they would have to talk about something on the drive to her house, and she certainly didn't want him pressing her for more information about Kaleb.

"Foster care is no way to grow up," he shook his head. "I lived in and out of foster homes until I was twelve. I got lucky enough to get into the Big Brother program with Wade Scott. My life has never been the same since. I wish every kid could have that experience," his eyes started to tear up. Jessie felt uncomfortable watching a grown man cry. She turned her head to look out the window, trying to give Bradley his privacy. Much to her relief, they didn't speak for the remainder of the ride. She was still trying to make the connection to his face. Where had she seen him before?

When they pulled into her neighborhood, she asked him to park a couple of blocks away, since she didn't want any questions from Mrs. Moore. She was supposed to be at the library. Bradley complied without questioning her motives.

"It was nice to meet you Jessie…I'm sorry. I didn't catch your last name."

"Watson. Jessie Watson is my name." She was already out the door before she finished her sentence, so she didn't notice his eyes widen and his mouth drop open as if he were going to say something but couldn't.

***

The days stretched slowly toward summer and graduation. During that time, Jessie gave into Shane's constant urging for her to experience a little more of the world before graduation. He was adamant that she should have a few good memories of her senior year of high school. Gradually, Jessie became more comfortable around his friends. At first, they seemed to accept her only because of Shane, but over time, they became her friends as well.

Jessie began to think of Shane as her long-lost brother. She laughed at the slow transformation that had taken place in the last few weeks. She had gone from his secret admirer to his sister. Shane was very protective of her, although she didn't completely understand why he seemed so attached to her. Maybe it was her mysterious connection to Kaleb that drew him to her.

When the last school dance drew near, Shane convinced one of his friends, Mitch, to ask her out. Mrs. Moore was ecstatic about the prospect of Jessie going on a date to a school dance and offered to go shopping with her for a new dress. Jessie declined, since she'd already agreed to go with Nikki.

Jessie and Mitch doubled with Shane and Nikki. They went bowling, which Jessie had never done before. At one point, she accidentally threw the ball backwards, narrowly missing Mitch. Instead of feeling self-conscious, as she was prone to feel, she laughed right along with the others. They ate dinner at one of Shane's favorite restaurants, a '50's style diner. Mitch and Shane dropped the girls off at Nikki's house, so they could get ready for the dance. Nikki transformed Jessie's long hair into beautiful braided twist. Her pastel yellow empire waist dress complimented her hazel eyes and fair skin.

The dance far exceeded Jessie's expectations. She had been nervous because she didn't know the first thing about dancing, but Mitch proved to be the perfect partner. He was a very experienced dancer, and he led her around the dance floor in the same manner as a prince would lead his princess. She liked the touch of his skin against hers, and the smell of his cologne. Once while they were dancing, she glanced up into his eyes, noticing for the first time how much they reminded her of Kaleb. Her imagination wrapped itself around that thought all too easily. When she felt Mitch's breath on her face, she was reminded of the time Kaleb had reached for her hand. She felt only a puff of air. Now she imagined Mitch's breath was Kaleb gently kissing her forehead. Then her thoughts shifted back to the present. She wasn't going to ruin her only dance dreaming of someone who wasn't real.

Jessie was a stranger to fast dancing. Mitch tried to teach her a few moves, but she looked more like a tin man in need of some oil. Mitch went with the flow, trying to mimic her moves instead. Before she knew it, a whole crowd of teens was dancing in the same mechanical way. She flashed a bright smile at Mitch, and she realized how handsome he was. He had the same blue eyes as Kaleb, but he had disheveled black hair that fell into loose curls where it hung slightly over his ears. Just before the fast song ended, Mitch approached her.

"Hey, do you want to get something to drink?" he asked above the noise of the blaring song.

"Sure," she took his hand as he led her off the dance floor toward the refreshment table.

"Not bad out there," he complimented her on her robotics.

"Whatever," she said, rolling her eyes at the misplaced compliment.

"I'm not kidding. You've got everyone doing it. Look," he motioned toward the dance floor, and sure enough, they were still mimicking her pathetic attempt at dancing as the screaming rhythm of the song increased in tempo. She couldn't help but laugh.

"I'm so glad you came with me tonight, Jessie," he said as he turned back toward her, "I'm glad I got a chance to get to know you better. I'm having a great time, and I can't remember when I've ever laughed as much as I have with you." He grabbed her hand and escorted her back to the dance floor as the frenzied mood of the fast song gave way to the soothing sounds of a love song. Mitch's blue eyes and dimpled smile danced with the melody of the music.

At that moment, Jessie was happy to be alive. She was experiencing butterflies in her stomach for the first time with someone who wasn't a figment of her imagination. She could feel the warmth of his hand around her waist, and the sweet compliments he spoke could be overheard by anyone who happened to be close by. This experience was real in every sense of the word.

The evening ended far too soon. Mitch gave her a hug before he left the Moore's front porch, and it wasn't the brotherly bear hug that Shane gave her either. It was the tender embrace of two people whose friendship had blossomed in a few short hours together – a hug that seemed to end with a comma rather than a period, as if it wasn't quite sure it wanted to be finished just yet. Jessie floated back in her room, sighing happily. She made a sign with a magic marker that read, "Thank you!" and taped it to her window for Shane. She sat in her room for a while, not wanting to get out of her dress or wash her make-up off, fearing that if she did the moment would fade as well.

She eventually found herself on the deck, drinking in the fresh air and soft moonlight. She knew Kaleb wouldn't come, but she always kept a small flicker of hope alive. Graduation was next week, and she worried about all the unknowns her future held. Jessie sighed heavily again.

"So, you had a good time tonight?" Shane was already jumping the fence as he spoke. He had changed into jeans and a t-shirt.

"I really did. Thank you so much," she said.

"Don't thank me, Jessie. Contrary to what you may have conjured up in your silly little head, I didn't pay Mitch to take you out. He wanted to ask you," he reassured her.

"Well, if that was true, he never would have noticed me if you hadn't befriended me and taken me under your wing," she admitted gratefully.

"I hate how you always think of yourself as if you were a piece of coal, Jessie, instead of the diamond you are. I mean look at you. You are absolutely beautiful, and you always have been; you just don't know it. And

I'm not talking about your outward appearance either. You're beautiful on the inside too, in spite all you've been through. It's no wonder Kaleb must have liked you, and quit trying to sell yourself short there too. If only Kaleb could have seen you tonight, I'm sure he would have thought twice about leaving," Shane smiled at her. Her face was already a fuchsia color, the heat radiating from it as he embarrassed her with his praise. She wasn't used to being openly admired by anyone but Kaleb.

"Why are you still in your dress anyway?" he asked.

"Because right now I feel like Cinderella at the ball, and I'm afraid when I take it off, I'll wake up and realize it was all a dream," she confessed.

"You're a bona fide nut case!" he laughed, shaking his head at her.

"I wouldn't expect you to understand," she retorted.

"Jessie, have you thought about what to do after graduation?" his tone grew serious again. She could tell he was worried about her.

"Margaret said I could stay here for the summer or until she gets a new foster kid, and she's going to help me find an apartment for the fall."

"Margaret? I've never heard you call her by her first name before," Shane observed.

"You've helped me realize that I can't shut myself off from this crazy world, or I will always be alone. I've decided to open myself up a little bit," Jessie revealed.

"Glad I could of assistance," he joked. "Sorry to interrupt. You were saying?"

"I have a summer job with the parks and rec department, and I got into the university on an academic scholarship, so…that's it, I guess. What about you?"

"I've decided to stay local too. I figure I'll get an apartment with Mitch or Jason – exert my independence, you know?" He walked closer to her as he added, "Everything will work out, okay?" With that he reached over and gave her his infamous big brother bear hug. Then, he climbed back over the fence and disappeared into his house, apparently raiding the refrigerator. She finally went to bed because, as she had noted throughout her life, time never stood still to allow her to relish a fading moment a little longer. Time moved steadily forward and onward, and it was truly no respecter of persons. Kaleb would have agreed with her on that point.

***

Graduation day was upon her before she felt fully prepared to deal with its intrusion on her newly acquired sense of security. She wore her dress from the dance because she felt more self-confident when she wore it. Amidst all the pomp and circumstance, tears, and flying mortar boards, Jessie had a feeling of solemn disappointment. She thought she would feel a sense of relief and jubilation that she had finally graduated, but instead she merely felt the long arm of time firmly pushing her into the abyss of the future, robbing her of the joy of the present.

After the ceremony was over, she wandered through the crowd watching families congratulate their graduates, taking pictures and exchanging hugs. She felt a pang of self-pity. She finally found Margaret, a wide smile beaming across her plump face. Jessie spotted someone standing by Margaret's side, someone Jessie recognized, but never expected to see again. What was he doing here, and what did his mysterious appearance have to do with the excitement that now danced about in Margaret's eyes? Jessie paused, considering whether she should disappear into the throng of people crowded around her, but Margaret caught sight of her first, motioning for her to come over.

"Jessie! Jessie!" she called, her voice shrill with anticipation, "Jessie, congratulations," Margaret gave her a big hug. Jessie only half-heartedly hugged her back.

"Jessie, this is Mr. Bradley Scott," Margaret introduced her unexpected guest with enthusiasm, pushing her gently toward him.

"We've met once before," Jessie's reservations about the acquaintance were clear from her expression, but Margaret didn't seem to notice.

"Mr. Scott has some exciting news to share with you, Jessie. I know you don't have any plans until the graduation party tonight, so I thought now would be good time for him to talk to you," she suggested. What exciting news could Mr. Scott possibly have that involved her? Was it about Kaleb? Her heart skipped a beat at the thought of his name.

"Here?" Jessie asked looking around at the crowd noisily bustling about.

"No," Bradley finally spoke, "I thought we could go back to the Moore's house."

"I have some shopping to do, but I should be home before you leave for your party," Margaret chimed in as if it was perfectly normal to leave Jessie alone in the house with a strange man she barely knew.

"I'll give you a ride," Bradley offered, motioning in the direction of his truck. Jessie recognized the black Dodge Ram, which had unexpectedly transported her home once before. She headed in the direction of the truck with Bradley following closely behind her. She could feel his eyes boring a hole in the back of her head.

Neither of them spoke on the short drive to the house. He opened the door for her, and she walked tensely to the house, her mind swirling with a million questions. She fumbled with her key, trying to get the door unlocked quickly so she could get this over with. She showed him to the couch in the living room, and she sat in the recliner adjacent to the couch.

"Well, I'm sure I'm the last person you expected to see today," he said anxiously. She nodded in agreement.

"Jessie, what I'm about to tell you is going to be hard to believe," he began. What was it with the Scott's – first Kaleb, now Bradley? She distinctly remembered Kaleb using a similar phrase as a precursor to their first conversation. Did the Scott's do anything that normal people could believe? Then she wondered if he knew about Kaleb – his current situation was certainly hard to believe – but before she could finish her speculation, Bradley finally decided to enlighten her on the reason for his visit.

"I'd like to start by telling you my story," he said. This was all hauntingly familiar to her, an echo from the past. Again, Kaleb had said the same thing the day he introduced himself. This was getting odder by the minute – it was déjà vu with Bradley as a substitute for Kaleb. What implications would it have for her life this time?

"I don't know how much you know about me, so I'll start at the beginning. I was in and out of my mother's care for several years before the state finally took me away when I was ten years old. She had exposed me to alcohol and drugs and all sorts of stuff that a kid should never have to deal with. When I was twelve, I met Wade Scott through the Big Brother program, and in time, his parents decided to adopt me, which was the best thing that ever happened to me. I had my vices, but they were supportive of me. I had a good life.

"A few years ago though, I heard about my biological mother's death through a lifelong friend. I decided to go to the funeral in an attempt to finally forgive her and free myself from all the anger I had bottled up inside for all those years. While I was at the funeral, I found out that my biological mother had another child long after I had been adopted.

"I discovered that the child, a little girl, had been taken away from her when she was a toddler. I knew if she hadn't already been adopted that she was being bounced around in the foster care system. I became obsessed with finding her, but I couldn't get any information about her besides what I already knew: her approximate age and her last name. I wasn't even sure what state she was in because my biological mother moved around so much. I was frustrated that I couldn't do anything. I had buried the rage, disappointment, and pain of my youth, compacting it beneath a solid mountain of sheer determination to change who I had been before the Scott's rescued me. Unknowingly, I had created a volcano, ready to erupt at any moment given the right circumstances and pressure. When I couldn't help my sister, all of my hate and anger suddenly exploded. I didn't know how to deal with all the emotion, so I tried to drowned it with alcohol.

"I had been out drinking late one night, and I thought I was sober enough to drive myself home. I hit a young woman dressed in dark clothes who was in the crosswalk. Thankfully, her injuries weren't fatal, but I ended up in jail over the incident for two years – two long years." Jessie shifted uncomfortably in her seat. She couldn't understand why he was pouring his heart out to her, but he was too intent on telling his story to notice.

He continued, "I felt like I had let down everyone who was important to me – my sister, my brother, my nephew, and my parents. It was a crossroad in my life, and I'm happy to say that I changed for the better in that two years. I learned how to deal with my anger through anger management classes. I completed AA, and I swore then that I would never drink again. When I got out of jail, my brother, the saint that he was, gave me a job at his company, and I tried to rebuild my life, never forgetting about my sister. My endless queries to the state turned up nothing. There was some garbage about updated computer systems and road block after road block. Then, my brother and his wife died in the car accident. I lost the only family I had left when Kaleb took off. I was alone, again, until I met you, Jessie." He looked up at her as he paused briefly. "Jessie, my sister is eighteen, and her last name is Watson."

Jessie was stunned. This was almost more unbelievable to her than Kaleb's story. She had a brother, and it was Bradley Scott? Her mind was reeling – she couldn't make sense of it. Bradley was trying to assess her reaction, but she simply stared at him blankly. He wanted to give her some time to process the information, and when she didn't say anything after a few minutes, he decided to leave her alone. He rose to go, but she called out, "Wait. Don't go. I'm sorry. I– I – I don't know what to say. I cannot believe that I have a brother." She fell silent again for several minutes.

"Are you sure?" she stammered.

"I'm positive. I've spent every waking minute since you told me your last name verifying all the information. Margaret has been more than helpful – it was actually through her that I got any information at all."

"So, what happens now?"

"Well, that's entirely up to you, Jessie. You're a legal adult, so you can do whatever you want. I know Margaret hasn't had a chance to tell you herself, but she found out today that she's getting another foster child next week. She didn't know what to do since you were planning on staying with her through the summer, but I want you to know that you'll always have a place with me. I'll clear out a room for you, and you can come and go as you please. I'll help you pay for college…whatever you need, Jessie. I've spent the last six years looking for you, imagining how I would introduce myself and what you would look like. I just want a chance to get to know you – a chance to show you what it's like to have a family, even if it's just me." As his voice trailed off, Jessie was struck with the sudden realization that she recognized him the first time they met because his face was a mirrored reflection of her own. They had the same eye and hair color, and their features were strikingly similar.

"Since I seem to be out of a place to stay, I'd be more than grateful to stay with you," she replied. "All my life I've wanted to belong to a family, even if it is a one man show." Bradley was beaming.

"Let me know when you're ready, and I'll be by to pick you up," he said as he reached for the door knob. She nodded her head.

Jessie was still trying to process her feelings while she was getting ready for the graduation party. She was so overwhelmed with emotions that she felt numb inside. Slowly, the shock faded, and the numbness gave way to a sense of anticipation. She would finally belong to a family, and she couldn't overlook the mysterious Kaleb connection. Because of his appearance in her life, she had found her place in the world. She had become friends with Shane and now her brother had found her – a brother she hadn't known existed.

She was intrigued by the fact that Kaleb had altered because of his grief over his parents' death, which he blamed on his uncle. Now, the very person whom he had hated so fiercely was offering her a safe haven from loneliness. He was offering her a future that had been sealed from her until Kaleb had unlocked the gate. Kaleb's introduction into her life had set in motion a series of events that would change the course of her life forever. It was like a huge boulder rolling down a mountain at full speed, but instead of leaving a wake of destruction in its path, new life was springing up.

Jessie had undergone a complete metamorphosis since her arrival at the Moore's. Where she had once thought of herself as encapsulated in a tomb of hopelessness, she now found herself enveloped in the sweet embrace of hope. She could leave her childhood in the deserted wilderness with no regrets because she was entering adulthood in the splendor of the forest, teaming with life and new beginnings. She had once questioned how she could go on, but now she knew. The moon still gave its light on a clouded night with hope that the clouds would dissipate. A sick child smiled with the hope that he would be well again. The fight that caused the loss of a brother would be resolved with the hope of reconciliation. She could always hold onto her hope, and at that moment, her reality far exceeded her greatest hopes, except for one, but she would continue to hope for him as well. She certainly had nothing to lose.

***

Shane picked her up for the graduation party, and he was surprised by her uncharacteristically happy disposition. Graduation had seemed more like a precipice from which she was being pushed rather than a reason for celebration. He had begged her to go to the party, and now she seemed, well, high. The realization struck him with blunt force, and panic set it. He looked at her uncomfortably, though she barely seemed to notice his presence.

"Jessie, are you…okay?" he wondered tentatively.

"I'm better than ever!" she laughed gleefully, which seemed to confirm Shane's suspicion that she was on drugs. He tried to keep it light, though his fears were getting the best of him.

"Jessie, did someone slip something into your drink tonight?" he asked. She only laughed in response as if he had cracked a hilarious joke. He slowed the car down and pulled into a vacant parking lot.

"Jessie. I'm serious. Are you on something? Because you're not acting like yourself, and I'm honestly getting a little worried." Jessie turned to look him in the eye, and her soft smile had a calming effect on his nerves.

"Shane, you're not going to believe this when I tell you. It's like some fairytale – something that would never happen in real life, especially to me."

"Try me," he replied skeptically.

"Do you want the good news or the bad news first?"

"Let's go for the bad," he answered, bracing himself for the worst.

"Margaret is getting a new foster kid, so I have to move out this weekend," she said calmly. Shane was stunned, whether by the actual news or her calmness, he wasn't sure.

"Now back to the bad news. You have to move out this weekend, and…you're okay with this?" he questioned, raising one eyebrow.

"Yeah," she said indifferently, shrugging her shoulders. He looked away, renewing his fear that she had done something drastic in response.

"Shane. I know what you're thinking! I am NOT on drugs!" She was disappointed in his lack of trust, and he was embarrassed that his thoughts had been so transparent.

"Do you want to hear the good news?" she asked, punching him in the arm.

"Go for it," he said, eager to hear the yin to the yang.

"I got the best graduation present ever – a brother!" she announced.

"What? Jessie, you've gone mad. You've snapped. Maybe I should take you home now," he said, puzzled by her seriousness.

"I told you that you wouldn't believe me, but I'm not kidding – and you'll NEVER guess who it is!" She was going to keep him in suspense.

"Let me take a stab at it…Brad Pitt? Matt Damon? The President of the United States?" he said sarcastically.

"Bradley Scott," she interjected. Shane's jaw visibly dropped open in complete disbelief. Jessie thought his eyes might bug right out of his head. He was too stunned to speak, so Jessie launched a full-scale explanation of her afternoon aboard the shuttle *Discovery*.

"This is too weird," he muttered. She finally managed to convince him that she was telling the truth and that she was moving in with Bradley this weekend.

"Jessie, are you going to feel awkward moving in with a single guy you don't know?" She had to admit that he had a valid point.

"I've thought about that a lot since he left, but you know he would be more like a father figure to me. I mean he's twenty years older than I am, and it's no more awkward than moving into a new foster home, I guess," she responded.

"Well, I'm truly speechless. How do you congratulate someone on being found by her long-lost brother? You know – awkward would be Kaleb showing up again only to find out his crush is really his uncle's sister. You'd be his aunt!" Now Shane was laughing, but Jessie was not. She honestly hadn't thought of that.

"Shane, it's not like they are related by blood you know. Bradley was adopted, and I'm only his half-sister at that," she glowered at him. She sounded like she was trying to convince herself, and Shane hadn't meant to strike a nerve. He didn't know how deeply rooted Jessie's feelings for Kaleb really were.

"Hey, I'm sorry. Can't you take a joke?" he said apologetically. Of course, she would forgive him, and she wouldn't let his "joke" affect her mood tonight. After all, she now had something to celebrate: the commencement of a new life.

Chapter 8: Love

Love

Love cushions the heart-felt dreams,
Love comforts the dying screams.
Love surrounds the longed-for peace,
Love's sweet embrace shall never cease.

Love protects a lost one's heart,
Love acts out the leading part.
Love heals those stricken with grief,
Love is the only durable relief.

Love imparts a story lost,
Love eases the emotional cost.
Love is the binding power,
Love is trust and hope that will never cower.

~ Jessie Watson

Bradley lived in a small two-bedroom, two-bathroom house. He had cleared the second bedroom out for Jessie. A large living room housed a huge flat screen television, black leather furniture, consisting of a recliner, a sofa, and a love seat, and of course a stereo system, complete with surround sound. A small den was nestled off to the side of the living room, where Bradley kept his computer and his personal library. The walls were painted a neutral tan color, contrasted with white molding, trim, and doors. The beautiful hardwood floor added to the character of the house. Jessie was surprised to see the large gourmet style kitchen. The dining area opened onto a beautiful deck, which was surrounded by a large open yard with huge trees shading the entire area.

"I've completely remodeled this place over the years. I've done most of the work myself with the help of Wade and Kaleb, of course, when they were around," he announced as he gave her a tour, a hint of pride in his voice. Jessie's heart roared to life at the thought that Kaleb was somehow part of this house.

"It's beautiful," Jessie commented.

"Your room is this way," he said as he led her to the end of the hallway. The room smelled of fresh paint, and Jessie gasped as she peered inside. The room had been painted in a muted sage green, her favorite color. An antique-looking dresser and matching vanity in a pale cream color lined the wall, which she later found out belonged to Kaleb's grandmother. She could hardly believe her eyes. The twin-sized bed was covered with a beautiful comforter that complimented the sage and cream color scheme.

"Bradley, you shouldn't have gone to all this work…how did you know my favorite color?"

"Margaret has your file," he said sheepishly. Of course, Margaret would have helped. Jessie was beginning to like Margaret more and more.

"Did you do this all yourself?" she asked, sensing that the place had a woman's touch. It certainly wasn't the bachelor pad she was expecting.

"Nah, I had some help," he smiled.

"How can I ever thank you? You've done too much," she praised him. She was surprised to see his face redden. Her compliment had embarrassed him. *Uncanny how alike we are,* she thought.

"You deserve it, Jessie," he said as he walked out of the room, so she could unpack. She wasn't used to being catered to, but she could certainly get used to this. Bradley was full of surprises. She wasn't quite sure why she had pegged him as a ruffian at their first meeting, aside from the fact that she had been terrified at his unexpected appearance. While she knew the cliff-note version of his life story, she didn't really know him. She quickly remedied that through observation.

Bradley was a great cook, thus the gourmet kitchen. He promised to teach Jessie how to cook, since she didn't know the first thing about it. He told her that cooking was one way he relieved stress. His taste in music covered a broad range from instrumental to heavy metal. He was an avid reader, and he loved playing sports, especially golf. He was also a Wii fanatic. He seemed to be an All-American guy, so Jessie couldn't help wondering why he wasn't married.

On her third night, her curiosity won out. After finishing a delicious dinner of chicken cordon bleu, baked sweet potatoes, and spinach and apple salad, Jessie was clearing the table while Bradley loaded the dishwasher.

"Bradley, do you mind if I ask you a personal question?"

"Not at all."

"Hasn't there ever been . . . a woman in your life?" Jessie felt stupid prying into his personal life.

"Well, yeah," Bradley didn't seem offended. "I've been dating Marci, the secretary at work, for quite a while, off and on, anyway – I guess we're coming on seven years now. She's the one who helped me with your room, and the decorating for the whole house, come to think of it."

"Why don't you get married?" she asked pointedly.

"I seem to have a problem losing the people I love. I guess I figured if I kept her at a distance maybe I wouldn't strap a death sentence to her," his voice was filled with melancholy. Jessie didn't know how to respond; she hadn't been expecting his answer.

She hadn't met anyone like Bradley before. He wasn't afraid to reveal his emotions, even if it meant crying in front of a complete stranger as he did when he was driving her home after their initial encounter. His sensitivity to the needs of everyone around him, from his friendly conversations with the cashiers at the grocery store to his carrying fast food gift cards in his glove box for those begging on street corners, emphasized the fact that he had the biggest, kindest heart. She wondered if he had always been like this, or if the jail time and the accident had acted as catalysts because he was the most selfless person she knew. She wished she was more like him.

Before meeting Bradley, Jessie tended to focus on the dark hole she'd been cast into while alienating herself from the rest of the world for something it had neither instigated nor condoned. Society in its way had tried to rescue her from the world Bradley had been subjected to while living with their mother. She had been spared in many ways from the abuse and neglect she otherwise would have received. She had never thought of her life in those terms before, and the thought was refreshing.

While she had never felt truly loved, at least she had been cared for, and that was a form of love. She imagined how hard it must have been for couples to open their hearts to a child only temporarily entrusted to them –

to form attachments would only bring heartache later as the child was moved for one reason or another. Sure, she'd seen her share of unkind foster families, but she'd also been in homes where the couple tried to make her feel included. She always pulled away. She suddenly realized that, like Kaleb, she too had chosen not to allow others to bond to her strand. She chose to live in isolation and loneliness rather than to have at least intermittent spurts of love or acceptance now and again. She had withdrawn from anyone who tried to reach out to her, just as she had done with Shane after first meeting him. Her recoiling had been a subconscious, almost an instinctive way to protect herself.

She had judged Kaleb harshly because he severed his bonds to his family, but she had been no better. She had reacted exactly the same way – she had withdrawn. Is that what he meant when he told her that he thought she of all people would understand how he had reacted? This epiphany was a recurrent topic of pondering over the next few days while she was mowing lawns, planting flowers, changing sprinklers, and emptying garbage cans for the parks and rec department. She concluded on Friday that she couldn't sit back and hope anymore. She decided to talk to Bradley about Kaleb after dinner.

***

"Bradley, I wasn't completely honest with you when we first met in the woods," she clarified as she sat down on the loveseat.

"Oh?" Bradley raised an eyebrow as he fixed his gaze away from the television and onto Jessie, intently listening. She hoped she was making the right choice trying to bring Kaleb back. She knew she was driven by selfishness, or rather consumed by a deep desire for her life to come full circle. Kaleb had been the starting point, weaving her strand back into the web of humanity masterfully, although he was fully unaware of how his appearance had affected her life. No, she wouldn't waver. She was determined to bring him back if possible.

"I met Kaleb this year," she said, preparing herself for the worst reaction.

"You what? Where is he?" Bradley demanded, and she was surprised at how angry he sounded.

"I don't know where he is now. He left. He said that he'd gotten too close to me. The last time I saw him was three weeks before you found me on his property," she answered, regretting her decision to pursue this. She couldn't tell Bradley the absolute truth – that no one could see Kaleb – that he didn't exist as Bradley was imagining.

"Why tell me this now?" he snarled at her while trying to regain his composure. She was obviously pouring salt into an old wound. She hadn't meant to hurt Bradley by deceiving him. Jessie's eyes filled with tears, and Bradley's expression softened.

"I didn't know you then, but now that I do, I'm positive that Kaleb doesn't know how much he lost by leaving," she hoped Bradley understood what she was trying to say.

"Jessie, Kaleb was angry when he left. No one could dissuade him from placing the blame on me, and it was his rage that drove him away. When he's ready, he'll come back," Bradley sounded confident in his assessment of the situation.

"Bradley, you're wrong about that. The last time I saw him he told me that although he saw the world differently, what was done was done, and there was no turning back. He never said he didn't want to come back. I don't think he knows how. The strangest detail of this whole story is that while Kaleb never told me about you himself, it was only because of him that I found you or Shane. It's as if he was unconsciously guiding me to you. I've thought about this for a long time now, Bradley, and I think Kaleb is afraid of how he'll be received," she explained. She knew the last sentence was a lie, but she knew it would motivate Bradley to help her. If only Bradley knew how much more complicated the whole situation was. Jessie didn't know if Kaleb could come back, but he had once told her that he was the exception to the rule.

"What am I supposed to do?" Bradley asked, taking the bait she had set before him. Jessie had already thought this part through. No one had gone looking for Kaleb when he disappeared – they just let him go. While they may not have forgotten about him in thought, their inaction led Kaleb to believe that his plight was hopeless. Their inaction allowed him to sever his bonds with the conviction that when his parents died, he died too. He felt his life was nothing more than a memory. When people stopped coming around and trying to reach out to him, he became lost in that memory of what had been, which blinded him from clearly seeing that he could live on, honoring his parents' memory by his very existence. Jessie had recently come to that realization herself, and she hoped her conclusions were sound. She told Bradley that they had to somehow let Kaleb know that they were looking for him, that they wanted him to come back.

Bradley set to work trying to reclaim the last member of his family that death had seemed to overlook. He filed a missing person report, posted flyers all over town, and hired a private investigator. Jessie knew no one would ever find Kaleb, for Kaleb was nowhere to be found, but she hoped as they tried to bond with his now invisible strand that it might rematerialize, if his strand was truly lost at all. Kaleb had told Jessie that he couldn't see the strands of Bradley and Shane, so maybe he was only temporarily blinded from seeing his own strand as well. She only hoped that he could feel their pull even if he couldn't see it, but surely, he could still see her strand. He couldn't have abandoned her completely.

The days turned into weeks, and the clock ticked on, counting the seconds, minutes, and hours of time that sped steadily forward like a railway train, never stopping but ever creaking along to its destination, a distant point far into the future. Bradley's hope waned as no new information was uncovered. The investigators were puzzled that Kaleb seemed to have vanished into thin air, leaving nothing behind except the stone-cold path of his life that abruptly ended with his parents' funeral. Jessie, however, was prepared for this, and she continued to hope that time would lead Kaleb home – time, persistence, and love. Surely, a love as deep as hers could call him back home. He couldn't sever her bond to him, even if he tried, even if he didn't feel the same in return.

Shane hadn't accepted her deceit as readily as Bradley. He was angry that she hadn't told him the truth about seeing Kaleb so recently, but he also knew that she hadn't wanted to betray Kaleb's trust. He was more hurt at the thought of Kaleb not coming to him. After all, he had been his friend longer than Jessie. Jessie let Shane surrender to nurse his wounded pride. Eventually, he started coming around again. He couldn't stay away for long – he had become a part of their patchwork family.

***

Jessie had just stepped out of the shower after work on Monday. She dried her hair and was applying her make-up when she heard the phone ring. She hadn't seen Bradley's truck in the driveway when she walked home. Bradley had been in the habit of dropping her off and picking her up from work, but this week, he had been working long hours, so she had been taking the bus. She normally let the machine pick up, but she decided this call must be important since whoever it was kept calling back.

"Hello?" she answered the phone.

"Jessie, I'm glad you finally picked up," it was Bradley, but his voice was strained, almost frantic.

"Is something wrong?" she asked, her nerves causing nausea to suddenly wash over her.

"They found a body matching Kaleb's description." A body? A dead body? Her mind was swimming with questions.

"Is he alive?"

"Barely," came the whispered response. "He's at Mercy Medical Center. I'm on my way there now."

"What do you want me to do?" She had no way to get to the hospital in a reasonable amount of time.

"What do you want to do?" he asked. Of course, nothing was ever easy. Was she thinking that Kaleb would walk through the door one day announcing his return? Actually yes, that was exactly what she thought would happen, so naturally the opposite would occur. What did she want to do? Her hands were shaking, and her heart was racing. She had a nagging thought occur to her: What if Kaleb didn't know her? He had never known her before he altered, so what if he didn't remember her now? How would she cope? Would Bradley and Shane think she was a farce? How foolish she felt – how lost – how vulnerable!

"Jessie?" Bradley interrupted her internal turmoil.

"I don't know," her voice cracked. She started to cry, but she wasn't sure why. She was scared. What if Kaleb died?

"Jessie, call Shane. I've got to go – I'm here." There was nothing but dial tone. Jessie clicked the talk button and dialed Shane's number. Luckily, he answered the phone.

"Hello."

"Hey, Shane. Can you come over and get me? They found Kaleb's body. They're not sure if…" she tried to control her voice, but the tears broke through again.

"I'll be right there," Shane didn't need to hear the rest of her sentence. He was at her door in fifteen minutes flat. He didn't bother knocking. As he rushed in, he gathered Jessie up in his big bear hug.

"It's going to be okay, Jessie. Tell me what happened," he urged.

"I don't know anything. Bradley called and said they found a body matching Kaleb's description, but he was barely alive. He's at Mercy Medical Center," she regained her self-control as she spoke.

"So, they're not sure if it's him?" he implored.

"I guess not," she muttered.

"Well, let's go. Bradley will need you there either way," he said, grabbing her hand to escort her out the door. How had she ever been blessed with such a good friend as Shane? When they arrived at the hospital, they found Bradley filling out paperwork at the front desk.

"Bradley?" Jessie spoke as she approached her brother.

"Hey," his voice was hoarse, and his eyes were red. Jessie knew he had been crying. She couldn't imagine how he was feeling – the last of his Scott family lying on a hospital bed, dying, and it was all her fault. She hadn't anticipated this. She found consolation in the thought that seeing Kaleb one last time was better for Bradley than never seeing him again, wondering the rest of his life what had become of him. Jessie tried to swallow the lump in her throat, but was it better for Kaleb? Surely, Kaleb was stronger than that – he could come back – he would come back. She found no solace in her reassurance. Jessie and Shane sat in the waiting area while Bradley finished. He finally joined them after what seemed like an eternity.

"The park ranger found the body at the property this afternoon. No one knows what happened or how long he was there. It doesn't look like an assault – no bruising, broken bones, nothing. He seems to be in a coma, so now we have to play the waiting game," his voice was gruff and strained with worry. He had spent far too long in this hospital himself, and he wasn't sure how he could bear to watch his nephew experience the same thing.

"Can we see him?" Shane asked the question. Jessie thought it was ironic that Shane phrased the question that way. A day ago, Shane literally wouldn't have been able to see Kaleb if he'd been standing right in front of him. What price did Kaleb have to pay to be seen again? What would it cost his family to see him again?

Jessie was so wrapped up in her thoughts she didn't notice Shane and Bradley get up. She had spent so much time in her own head throughout her life that she had learned to automatically tune the rest of the world out.

"Jessie," Bradley tapped her arm gently, jarring her back to reality, "are you coming?" She rose to her feet and followed Bradley with Shane by her side. Her body was trembling like an autumn leaf about to plummet from its home in the trees with a passing breeze. She had to focus on putting one foot in front of the other. She entered Kaleb's room timidly, hiding behind Shane's muscular frame. She was suddenly afraid to see him again, afraid he would be angry at her for forcing him to come back. Maybe she had overanalyzed the situation and misinterpreted his true motives. Doubt had a way of destroying the strongest of convictions like a wrecking ball tearing down a sturdy stone wall.

She peeked around Shane as they approached the hospital bed. A sudden jolt of pure joy swept through her at the sight of him, hearing the monitor loudly beep with each heartbeat. She knew now how Geppetto must have felt when he first saw Pinocchio as a real boy. Kaleb looked angelic lying there at death's door. He was more handsome in person than she remembered, and her memories were more than generous to his features. His hair was still tousled in the same way it had been when she last saw him. It was almost as if he stood frozen in time, oblivious to the sweeping changes that had occurred around him.

No one said anything for quite some time; the three of them simply stared in awe that Kaleb was really back. They all blinked slowly, fearing that he may vaporize in the instant their eyes had been closed. Each one was contemplating a thousand questions he or she would like to ask him. Each one was trying to squelch the unspoken fear that Kaleb may never wake up. Shane finally leaned over Kaleb's still body, giving him a hug as best he could while whispering, "Hey buddy – it's me, Shane. I'm glad you're back. I've missed you. We have a lot of catching up to do, not to mention I'm going to beat the crap out of you for leaving like that." Shane tried to laugh at his own joke, but the laugh got stuck in his throat, sounding more like a muffled moan.

Bradley didn't say anything. He wasn't quite sure if his presence would help or hurt Kaleb at this point. Jessie could understand his concern, but she felt so strongly that Kaleb needed to know Bradley was there. She didn't think that Kaleb's return could erase the influence of the watchers, with whom he saw the world from a different perspective – a higher plane. She felt that his experience as a watcher was fused to his soul, whether he could remember the last three years or not. If he returned, he would return as her Kaleb, not as the Kaleb engulfed in rage and hopelessness. She didn't know how she knew, but she knew.

All eyes were on Jessie now. She hesitated, still worrying about whether Kaleb would recognize her, and if he did, how he would react to her. She stepped from behind Shane's shadow, wishing they would leave her alone with him for a moment. She couldn't stall any longer. She didn't touch him, but she hovered by him for a minute before she said, "Kaleb, it's Jessie – I

– I'm glad you're back. I've got a story of my own that you're not going to believe, but I'm not going to tell it to you until you wake up." She couldn't say anything else in the presence of her silent audience, whose eyes were still on her as if they were expecting Kaleb to miraculously wake up at the sound of her voice. She would be the first to admit that she had wished for the exact same impossibility.

Shane's face was housing a huge grin as he said, "Uh, Jessie, you have to kiss him if you want to wake him up!" Both he and Bradley burst into laughter as Jessie's face turned bright red. Leave it to Shane to keep the atmosphere light. Perhaps he was a little too laid back about everything.

"Shut up, Shane. He's not Sleeping Beauty," Jessie said stifling a smile, although she added in her head, *"but he certainly could be the Prince."* Shane's humor broke the tension in the room, and they relaxed. Time dragged on, and there was no change in Kaleb's condition. Shane left two hours later. After the nurse assured Bradley she would call if there was any change, he decided to go home as well, and he urged Jessie to go with him to get some sleep, but she couldn't leave Kaleb. If he woke up, she didn't want him to be alone. Bradley didn't force the issue.

Jessie's eyes drifted around the sterile hospital room to avoid focusing on Kaleb's seemingly lifeless body, although she certainly could have stared at his face all night long without tiring of his features. She jumped when she saw him. It was Kaleb, her invisible Kaleb, hunched in the corner with his head in his hands. The hair on her arms stood straight up as a chill ran through her body. She shuddered.

"Kaleb?" she whispered. No response.

"Kaleb?" she whispered again. Still no response. She had done this to him. She had torn him in two. He had to make the decision to come back, and he didn't want to. What had she done? She touched the arm of Kaleb's body – the first time she had been able to touch. She gently put his hand in hers. Her stomach fluttered, and she shuddered again. She had imagined this moment over and over, but the magic wasn't there because her Kaleb wasn't there. As she touched his hand, her Kaleb looked up in response. She whispered, "Kaleb, I love you. We all love you – Bradley and Shane too. We need you to come back. Please come back to me. I'm so sorry…I'm sorry." Then her Kaleb was gone, vanished into thin air. It was Déjà vu yet again, but this time Jessie was offering the apologies.

She noticed no change in the rigid form lying in the hospital bed. She began to cry. As she released her tears, she felt the weight of eighteen years of loneliness slowly lift from her. She wasn't alone anymore because of Kaleb. Exhaustion finally overcame her. She pulled her chair close to the bed, placing her hand on top of his. She curled up as best she could and fell asleep.

Interlude 5

Valeressa was drawn out of her trance by a motion she caught out of the corner of her eye. Kaleb's body was disappearing and reappearing sporadically. Valeressa sat up in alarm. She had been in stasis longer than ever. Days perhaps weeks by the time table of the other realm. She had no idea how long Kaleb's body had been zoning in and out of stasis. Something or someone must have been trying to pull it through to the other realm, and she was sure it was not Kaleb's doing. She did not bother to get Master Burdock's permission before she left. She had made up her mind, and nothing he said or did would stop her. She had to help Kaleb. As she stood up to leave, Kaleb's body disappeared altogether. She waited, but it did not return.

She searched for him everywhere in the watcher's realm, but he was nowhere to be found. She knew he had to be in the other realm, possibly reunited with his body, but she had to be sure. She stepped into the vortex, hesitantly. It had been three years since she had been in the other realm, and she was suddenly nervous. She focused her mind on Kaleb, hoping her connection to him was strong enough. She closed her eyes tightly and walked with Kaleb's face in her mind.

When she felt the pressure of the vortex dissipate, she finally opened her eyes. She recognized her surroundings as a hospital, though she could not see Kaleb anywhere. Had she only been transported to his body, or had she been transported to him? She began wandering around the facility, trying to sense his presence, but she was distracted by the insistent image of the man shoving his way to the forefront of her mind. Not now, she said to him, pushing the image away, but he immediately appeared again, begging for recognition. She surrendered to the pleading in his eyes, for just a moment, completely unaware that she was walking as she studied his face. She was oblivious to her surroundings until she found herself standing in a small hospital room in the long-term care wing.

It took her a moment to realize that she was looking at the owner of the face that had been haunting her all this time. There he was in the flesh with a little girl sitting on his lap looking at a book. The girl's bright red curls hung loosely around her shoulders. She looked at a picture and then pointed to the person lying in the bed. Valeressa took a step closer to get a better view. She gasped as she peered at herself lying in the bed. As the scene unfolded before her eyes, the pieces of her past fell into place. A four-year-old girl. The man whose face had led her here. Seeing his face only in the presence of Gage or Minnion.

As she watched, she had the urge to cry to release the increasing pressure inside of her. That face had a name, and she remembered it well. For four long years, Patrick had stayed by her side. He had raised their daughter into a beautiful little girl. He had remained constant and true, despite her condition, despite the bleakness of her future. All this time she had thought no one loved her. She had wrestled with the loneliness that perched on her shoulder, but she could never quite get the right hold on it. She realized that it hadn't been loneliness at all. She had been homesick, and the nagging feeling was her longing to return to those she loved. Patrick's laughter penetrated her thoughts. He was laughing at something the little girl had said. She suddenly remembered why she had come to the hospital in the first place.

She rushed from the room in a frantic search for Kaleb. She found him easily enough. He was crouched in the corner of the hospital room where his body lay, his hands covering his head as if he were in deep agony. She grabbed him, jerking him to his feet.

"Snap out of it, Kaleb!" she said pointedly.

"What are you doing here?"

"I came to find you – to stop you from doing something rash, but I found something on the way I need to show you." She hurried down the hall with a confused Kaleb in tow. When she reached the room, she pushed him inside. Kaleb stared, stunned at the seemingly

lifeless figure on the bed, his eyes shifting from the man and girl to Valeressa's body.

"Kaleb, I need to talk to you. Will you come with me back to the watcher's realm?" she asked, but he only stared at her in disbelief that here in the same hospital both of their lives hung in the balance.

"Kaleb?" He did not respond, but he followed her as she opened the vortex for both of them.

"Kaleb, I have a confession to make. That night you altered, Master Burdock sent me back to the other realm to retrieve your body. I wasn't allowed in the other realm in part because I was not as attuned to the vibrations of the web as a watcher needs to be, but also because I can touch things in the other realm. You could not fully alter because you had severed ties to the other realm, so your body was left behind. I was entrusted with the task of caring for your body by keeping it in stasis, a place that exists between both realms that only I can access. I never told you because Master Burdock forbade me. He said you must make the choice on your own whether to go or to stay, and it would make no difference whether you knew about stasis or not.

"Kaleb, you need to let go of your past and embrace your future. That girl back there loves you. You can tell just by looking at her. She reattached you to the web, so strong, so powerful is her love for you. You made your choice to stay in the watcher's realm, but she has also made her choice to keep you in her realm. Kaleb, she knows all about you, and she loves you still. Wake up and quit wallowing in your own self-pity. You have a unique opportunity at your fingertips. People in the watcher's realm don't often get second chances. Don't throw yours away." She had never spoken to any of the watchers in such a manner, but the present situation demanded it.

"So why exactly are we going back to the watcher's realm, and what was all that back there with you?" Kaleb finally asked as they approached the end of the vortex.

"I have some business to take care of. I just needed to get that off my chest first, so I knew I had done everything in my power to prevent you from making a mistake. You're free to go back if you want." He, however, did not turn back, whether out of curiosity

about what she was about to do or to delay his decision, she did not know nor did she ask. He followed her as she scoured the area for Gage and Minnion. She finally spotted them and marched forward, shouting their names in anger. Having never witnessed an angry outburst within the realm before, everyone in the vicinity halted and gathered around the foursome. The tone and volume of Valeressa's voice even summoned Master Burdock from wherever he had been absorbed in the ebb and flow of the web.

"Why didn't you tell me?" she reached out to grab Minnion, but Gage blocked her way. Minnion cowered under her angry glare.

"Minnion? What is she talking about?" Gage asked.

"You knew the whole time, and you didn't tell me," she raged.

"I didn't know the whole time. I only recognized you when I brought Kaleb to see you that first time. I didn't know before then, I promise," Minnion's voice was barely audible.

"But you knew when I talked to you after Gage came to see me. You knew then, and you said nothing!"

"But I couldn't take it back. I couldn't send you back. I couldn't undo it, so I took your advice. I left it in the past."

"It wasn't your past to leave behind. It was mine."

"But to make you suffer – to know what I had been about to do to you. I couldn't bear to have you think of me like that. You could finally see me for who I really am – deep inside. You told me I had a gift. I didn't want you to remember who I was. I didn't want to disappoint you again. Don't you understand yet? You were the only one in the other realm who saw passed all that – the only one who kept giving me a chance. You were my advocate like I was Kaleb's, and I couldn't bear to disappoint you again. What difference would it have made if I had told you then anyway? It's not like you can go back. It's like you said, I can't undo it."

"It makes all the difference in the world Isaac because I'm still alive!" She stopped herself. Isaac? Yes, his name had been Isaac in the other realm. She had been his social

worker. That's why everyone navigated toward her. In the other realm, she helped kids just like them. She remembered it all now – the dark parking lot, the figure jumping from behind the bush, her last thoughts of the baby who was due in three weeks, her husband, Patrick. She remembered it all. She took a step backward and stumbled, but Kaleb broke her fall.

"Minnion, would you please tell me what's going on?" Gage demanded.

"She was the pregnant woman I was trying to attack the night you intervened," Gage shot a glance at Master Burdock, who had been watching the exchange in silence. His expression did not change at the revelation. Minnion continued, "She was my social worker."

"Why would you attack her?" Gage asked.

"I overheard her tell someone that she was assigning my case to another social worker. I thought she was abandoning me like everyone else. I ran away before she saw me, and I hid for two days. I cried for a while, and then my sadness turned to anger. I got angrier by the minute, and I decided that if I couldn't live, then neither should she."

"So how did she end up here?" Gage wondered aloud. For the first time, Master Burdock spoke up.

"She got entangled in the vortex when you grabbed for Minnion. She had attached herself to his strand though his attachment to her was not substantial enough to hold him in the other realm. However, the strength of her attachment to him pulled her through the vortex. Because she was so securely attached to the web and because Minnion altered at the same time, I did not see what happened. So Valeressa, your body remained behind in the other realm, thus you retained the ability to touch in the other realm. Your attachments were trying to pull you back to them, thus your blackouts. Your heart is pure, innocent, and compassionate in both realms, thus everyone is magnetized toward you."

"You knew?" Valeressa asked, stunned.

"Not until now. Not until now."

"I'm sorry, Master Burdock," Gage said. "I should have come to you, but I didn't know that could happen, and I didn't know Valeressa was the woman. I never saw her face." Gage hung his head in shame.

"Gage, we must all make difficult choices. You did what you thought best, and you saved three lives that night. Do not apologize," Master Burdock's voice was a soothing balm over Gage's aching heart.

"It's me who should apologize," Minnion said flatly. "I'm the cause of all of this. I never deserved to be here in the first place. I don't belong here anymore than I belonged there." His melancholy tone, the desperation and hopelessness in his face, extinguished the angry flame in Valeressa's heart, and she remembered how much she loved Isaac, how difficult his life had been. She walked toward him, but he refused to meet her eyes.

"Isaac," she said, placing her hands on his shoulders. "Isaac, please look at me." He complied reluctantly. "Isaac, I love you. I have loved you since the day I was assigned your case file." There was no doubt in his mind that she spoke the truth. Deep down, he had always known that. "You were assigned to another social worker because I was going on maternity leave. It was only temporary, and I fully intended to keep in touch with you. I didn't know you had overheard my conversation with my supervisor, and then you disappeared. You didn't come home from school that day, and I thought you had run away. It was a misunderstanding."

"But I would have hurt you, Dara. I wanted to hurt you," he whispered. Dara. Yes, Dara was her name.

"I forgive you, Isaac, but you're wrong about one thing," she looked at Kaleb, who stepped forward.

"You do belong here, Minnion," Kaleb affirmed.

"Yes," Master Burdock echoed. "You do belong here, young Minnion."

"But I withheld the truth from you Master Burdock, surely –"

"Minnion," Master Burdock interrupted, "you fall under the special circumstances category with your friends here. Yet another exception. You saw Gage for the first time

only as he jumped between you and Valeressa because you were committing an act of desperation, having tried to cut yourself loose from the web. What makes your circumstance different from Kaleb's is that you were cutting yourself loose by physically severing the bond that held you there. Because she, your one connecting strand, was drawn into the vortex with you, you were able to alter into our realm without leaving your body behind. She was not fully able to alter because she is still fully attached to the web, just as Kaleb is. Kaleb's body, however, was held in stasis, so he was able to act as a watcher, while Valeressa's body was always in the other realm. She could not feel the web as we do. Even Kaleb can't feel it as strongly as Gage and the others gathered here. So, you see Minnion, you are an exception. Had you altered as one normally should, you would have come to the knowledge you have gained here tonight much more quickly. Days instead of years. You would have felt Valeressa's love as strongly as she feels it, but she was suspended between both realms and as she was your attachment to the web, you could not feel the full effects of the web in that regard. Nor will you be able to until she chooses a realm in which to dwell permanently." Master Burdock was now looking at her as if to tell her she had a choice to make. She in turn looked at Kaleb.

"By the looks of things, Valeressa, I think we both have somewhere else to be right now," Kaleb said. "Our services are required within the web. It seems there are repairs to be made there that only we can make." Master Burdock smiled. Kaleb and Dara said their goodbyes and walked through the vortex together.

***

Jessie woke with a start. Bradley was staring down at her, and Kaleb was gone. She sprang to her feet, and Bradley grabbed her elbow to steady her. Her eyes were wide with disbelief.

"Relax. They needed to run some tests. He'll be back in an hour or so. I called your work to let them know you couldn't make it in today. Why don't you go home, change, and get something to eat?" he suggested.

"Marci is waiting for you in the lobby. She can take you home," Bradley didn't wait for Jessie to answer. He escorted her to the door. Jessie had never met Marci, who was a slender woman with sleek black hair cropped to her chin in an A-line cut. She had dark eyes, a splattering of freckles, and a warming smile. She was very pleasant, and Jessie immediately liked her. Marci dropped her off and left for work.

Jessie took her time showering and managed to eat a bowl of cold cereal to quiet her grumbling stomach. Thinking gave her a headache, so she finally succumbed to sleep again. She didn't hear the phone ring the first time, or the second time, or the third time, or the fourth time. She was dreaming, but in her dream, she couldn't permeate the darkness. She could see spots of light, but every time she reached one, the darkness would engulf it. She was desperately trying to escape the thick blackness. The sound of the doorbell ringing and violent pounding on the front door startled her awake too quickly. It took her a moment to get oriented before she remembered where she was. She ran to the door, unlocking it with fingers that suddenly felt as if they had been molded from gelatin.

"He's awake, Jessie! He's awake! Brad's been trying to call you all morning, but you wouldn't answer. Let's go!" Shane was pulling her out the door while he was talking. She broke free from his grip and dashed back inside to get her shoes. Shane was a bundle of nerves – Jessie had never seen him like this. He kept rambling on and on, not making any sense at all. She, too, was a bundle of nerves: excitement, anticipation, and trepidation all rolled up in one.

They raced to Kaleb's room, slowing to catch their breath before they entered. Again, Jessie cowered behind Shane, unsure and sick to her stomach. As Shane stepped in the doorway, she heard a loud exclamation, "Shane!" The sound of Kaleb's deep voice made her knees buckle – it had been so long since she had heard his voice. It was crisper, clearer somehow

– more resonant than she remembered. She recognized it nonetheless. Shane bounced forward to give Kaleb a hug like a big cat lunging for its favorite squeaky toy.

Jessie hung back, her heart nearly stopping as she caught her first glimpse of his face, which was wide awake and brimming with life. His eyes were bright and beaming like the sky on a hot summer day – no – like a bright blue lake reflecting the sun's light. His boyish grin was exactly the same. She couldn't believe it. Her heart was racing so quickly she thought she was going to pass out.

The room started to spin as a fireball suddenly engulfed her. Sweat began beading on her forehead. She backed slowly toward the doorway, one shaky step at a time until she cleared the door frame. Her knees gave way. Spots appeared in her vision, like the little spheres of light in her dream, and then the darkness engulfed her too.

A hundred little knives sliced through her nose as the smelling salts forced her eyes to snap open. She blinked several times in an attempt to clear her vision. Three faces stared down at her, forming a circle above her head: a nurse, Shane, and Bradley.

"If you had waited a few more seconds to come around, I might have convinced Kaleb only a kiss would wake you," of course Shane would break the uneasy silence with one of his wise cracks. Her pulse quickened at the mention of Kaleb's name, which was loudly noted by the nurse, much to the delight of Shane. Jessie blushed. She could feel the heat radiating from her face.

"Shane, leave her alone. I think she's had enough excitement for one day. A kiss might put her in cardiac arrest," Bradley chimed in as the laughter echoed down the corridor. Jessie rolled her eyes.

"Why don't you make yourselves useful and help me up?" she

responded. *Leave it to me to pass out,* she thought. They each grabbed an arm and pulled her to her feet. She steadied herself, still feeling light headed.

"We're headed to the cafeteria to get Kaleb something to eat. We'll pick you up some juice while we're at it," Bradley said, shooting a look in Shane's direction.

"Yeah, I'm sure four arms are better than two for carrying one tray," Shane quipped, but he followed Bradley down the hallway, raising his eyebrows up and down repeatedly as he walked by Jessie. She quit watching him as he started making kissing faces at her. That left her alone. She walked back into the room slowly with her eyes staring down at the white squares on the floor. When she finally managed to look up, Kaleb was smiling at her. He winked just as he had the first day they met. She let out a huge sigh of relief and walked to his bedside, never looking away from his eyes this time.

"Jessie," he said, "that was quite an entrance, or should I say exit?" She laughed, and his smile widened.

"I – I – wasn't sure if you'd remember me," she said softly, struggling to say the right words.

"Well, my memory is pretty foggy, but I remember your face very clearly – I remember you very clearly. It's like I've known you all my life, but I know I haven't," he tried to explain. She was somewhat relieved that he didn't remember everything – that he wasn't angry with her, but she was afraid their connection had been lost as well. He may remember her, but what did he remember? Did he still feel the same way about her? Did he still know everything about her? Did he remember their talks, the tutoring, the campus tour, and the driving lesson?

"And you and Bradley?" she asked.

"I feel so different somehow. I'm me, but I'm not me. I really can't explain it. I was never mad at Uncle Brad, really. I resented him for living when my parents died. I was a real jerk to him, and I have no right to expect any kindness from him. I'm lucky he's forgiving," he said. Had he been awake long enough for them to reconcile already?

"How long have you been awake?"

"About five hours now, I think."

"Five hours!" she exclaimed. Why hadn't Bradley called sooner, or maybe he had? She had no idea how many times he tried calling her before he got a hold of Shane.

"Bradley and I had a lot to talk about. I understand I have a new aunt," he said. She looked away. He was clearly defining their relationship now. He didn't love her or couldn't love her if Bradley was her brother. Maybe he only viewed her as a friend, and Bradley happened to be a lucky excuse to let her down easy.

"Yeah, pretty weird, huh?" she tried to hide her misery, but Bradley and Shane saved her from anymore awkward conversation with Kaleb. While Kaleb ate, she withdrew to a corner and sipped her juice, trying to pretend her heart wasn't shattering into little pieces with each word he spoke and each glance they exchanged.

Kaleb was released from the hospital two days later with a clean bill of health but no explanation of where he had been for the past three years. The doctor's claimed amnesia, but Jessie knew otherwise. Jessie returned to work the day after Kaleb woke up, trying to get back into a routine to push Kaleb out of her mind. That would not be an easy task, since he would now be living with Bradley too. Bradley moved his computer into the corner of the living room and boxed up his books to accommodate Kaleb's sleeping quarters.

Kaleb was at Bradley's house when Jessie got home from work on

Friday. She didn't hate or resent Kaleb; she loved him, but he obviously didn't return her affections. She wasn't sure how to bury the love, so they could at least be friends again. Avoidance wouldn't work since they lived under the same roof.

Dinner wasn't too uncomfortable since Kaleb and Bradley did most of the talking. Besides, Jessie enjoyed listening to the sound of Kaleb's voice – to his every inflection as he asked questions and to the cadence of his words as he articulated the dullest of words. He was trying to catch up on all that had happened during his three-year hiatus.

"Hey Uncle Brad, I was wondering if you could give me a ride to pick up my truck tomorrow. I remembering leaving it in the storage shed on the property. It should still be there," he said as Jessie began clearing the table. Jessie cringed at the words 'Uncle Brad'; she would never get used to Kaleb calling him that. She accidentally brushed up against his arm as she was reaching for his empty plate. Her stomach turned a somersault as she tried to suppress the deep longing that welled up inside her. She had dreamed so many times of holding his hand and being held in his arms, but now that he was real and close enough to touch, she couldn't. He wouldn't. He didn't seem to notice her reaction as she rushed off to the rinse the dishes in the sink.

"It's there, alright. I've been driving out there every week or so to run the engine for a bit. I'd take it for a spin every so often too, so it was in good driving condition when you came home," Bradley answered with a wink. "I'd be happy to give you a lift, and even happier to see you driving it again. Chauffeuring has never been among my aspirations."

As the conversation turned to truck talk and mechanics, Jessie excused herself from the table claiming she had a headache. She disappeared into her bedroom where she nursed her broken heart. She wasn't sure if she could take much more of this. Kaleb's presence was becoming her own personal nightmare. This was her bitter-sweet ending.

Jessie wasn't sure how to occupy herself on Saturday with Kaleb there. Maybe a long walk would do. Maybe she could forget to come home until Kaleb was asleep. *Yeah right,* she thought, *Bradley would have the police out in force searching for me.* Was everyone blind? Could no one see the torture she was being subjected to?

After breakfast, Bradley asked, "So Kaleb, are you ready to get your truck?"

"Sure thing," Kaleb replied, grabbing his shoes. Jessie was sulking in the corner pretending to read a book.

"How about it, Jessie, are you up for a drive?" Bradley asked, obviously not wanting her to feel left out since Kaleb's arrival.

"Nah, I'll hang out here," she said trying to sound distracted and aloof.

"Come on, Jessie. You need to get some fresh air," Kaleb interjected. Jessie scowled at him from behind her book as he threw her shoes toward her. She apparently had no choice, so she reluctantly laced up her shoes. Kaleb had hardly talked to her the last two days, why the sudden interest in her health?

While Bradley got in the driver's seat of the his truck, Kaleb opened the door for her, and she climbed into the passenger seat out of habit. The truck had an extended cab, and she could have easily fit in the back had she thought of it. Kaleb climbed in, squishing her into Bradley.

"Oh. I'm sorry. I can sit in the back, so we won't be so crowded," she offered, hoping to escape the smell of Kaleb's cologne and direct contact with his skin, which tended to give her noticeable goose bumps.

"I'm perfectly comfortable," Kaleb smiled at her. The wall of indifference she had been struggling to construct crumbled. This was going to be a long drive, a long day, a long summer, a long life. When they finally reached the storage barn, Kaleb hopped out and waited. Jessie stared ahead wondering what his hold up was because she was ready to be on her way and out of his.

"Well, are you coming or what?" he asked Jessie impatiently. She looked at him with surprise: *Was this an invitation?* He had practically ignored her for the past three days, and now he wanted her to spend some quality time with him? When she didn't move, Bradley nudged her with his elbow since she was all but sitting on his lap, and then pushed her out of the cab of the truck. Kaleb slammed the door shut, and Bradley drove away, leaving a cloud of dust behind him.

Jessie stood at the top of the hill looking at Kaleb warily, utterly speechless. *Had he developed some sort of Dr. Jekyll and Mr. Hyde syndrome? Were there serious side effects related to un-altering, if that's what it was called?* She was at her breaking point.

"Come on!" he called as he raced down the hill. She much preferred to watch his muscles flex as he moved. She hadn't noticed his muscular build before, so why did she have to notice it now?

"Come on," he shouted again, so Jessie sauntered down the hill. Now that they were finally alone together with no possible chance of interruption, maybe she could get all of her feelings off of her chest and be done with it. She owed herself that much relief. Kaleb was standing by the barn waiting expectantly, no doubt for the unveiling of his prized possession. He stood there not moving as she approached.

"What?" Jessie asked, not sure what she was supposed to be doing. Kaleb reached for her hand – déjà vu again – but this time she felt his firm grip around her fingers. Once again, her heart raced, her stomach turned a cartwheel, and she smiled at him, uncertainly. Had she just been angry with him a second ago? Her mind seemed clouded all of a sudden.

"I've been waiting to do this the right way – my way – not in a hospital room or in Uncle Brad's living room, but here…where it should have happened a long time ago," he said. Jessie's mind was a blur now, and she couldn't think of anything to say. She wanted to punch him for torturing her the last few days, but her joy overpowered her anger. Words couldn't capture the emotions she was feeling. He pulled her toward him, his eyes fixed on hers. He turned her so she was facing him, though she was sure he was trying to anchor her feet to the ground since it felt like she was floating in the air. He leaned in close to her face, closer still, until she felt his lips touch hers. She could feel his breath on her face. Her arms seemed to lift themselves up until they wrapped gently around his neck. His arms were at her waist, pulling her closer. She could feel his heart pounding in unison with hers – the same fast paced rhythm. Then he drew away, and she opened her eyes only to find him staring at her already.

"I love you, Jessie," his voice was sweet music to her ears.

"I…I…I was afraid you didn't…that you wouldn't…" she couldn't speak coherently. She could hardly catch her breath. He put his arms around her and hugged her close to him.

"I never meant to hurt you, Jessie. I don't remember exactly what happened, but I know I hurt you. I'm sorry." She only hugged him tighter, burying her head in his chest. After a few moments, she felt a little more grounded in reality.

She pushed him away and punched him in the arm, "You are a dirty, rotten weasel! Do you have any idea what you've put me through the last three days? And don't you ever call me your aunt again!" He laughed, and she wished she could bottle-up the sound so she could always hear it. Then, he grew serious again.

"Jessie, you remember everything, don't you?"

"Yes," she replied as he grabbed her hand again, leading her to a shady spot under a tree.

"Will you tell me, please?" he asked.

"I can't tell you how many times I've lied to keep your secret, and now I'm afraid you aren't going to believe me even though you told me the story yourself. You'll have to trust that I'm not imaginative enough to make this stuff up," she said.

He smiled as he brushed a long strand of hair out of her face with his fingers, "Try me."

They must have talked for hours, and it was like old times, except now Kaleb was there with her – for real. She could reach out and brush a bug out of his hair or trace her fingers along the palm of his hand. She wished once again that time could stand still so she could live in this moment forever. Kaleb readily accepted everything she told him. He told her it felt right as if something locked deep inside him knew the truth, but kept the truth from his own memory.

"Kaleb, how did you know to bring me here?" she asked.

"I'm not sure. When I saw you in the hospital, I had a flashback, a vague memory of being here with you. I remembered that I had tried to hold your hand, but for some reason I couldn't. I knew that this place was somehow special to us. Although, it's a good thing I don't remember you almost wrecking my truck," he joked. She punched him in the arm again. He couldn't stay serious for long. He reminded her of Shane in that regard.

"So how did you know I would come here with you? I mean you hardly talked to me that last few days. I was beginning to think I had the plague or something," she probed.

"Jessie, I heard you in the hospital the night before I woke up. I recognized your voice, but I was trapped. I couldn't move or talk. When you spoke, everything about you rushed back into my memory. When I felt you touch my hand, I wanted to pull you right next to me. I cannot describe the feeling, the yearning, I had to be near you. When I woke up, and you weren't there, I thought you were in my head. Then Bradley came in and told me that you were his sister. I was overwhelmed with everything, I guess. I didn't know how to respond, and I couldn't remember much about the last three years. I wasn't sure if I was imagining things. Then I wasn't sure what had really happened. I see and feel only bits and pieces it seems like, and those pieces are blurred.

"When I finally saw you at the hospital when I woke up, you didn't hug me or touch me at all. I was sure I had been dreaming the night before. I didn't know what to say to you. I was so confused. But when you brushed by my arm last night after dinner, I knew there was something between us that I had never felt before. I couldn't deny my feelings anymore. I wasn't getting anything from you but negative vibes, but Shane was always joking with you as if you liked me, so I decided to take a chance. I hoped beyond hope that my flashback had really happened. I guess it was a good gamble," he explained. She wondered what kind of turmoil she had put him through the last three days, keeping her distance, avoiding him. He thought he was crazy for loving her, and she thought he didn't care for her. How confusing it must have been for him, not knowing what was real!

"Well, we better get back before Uncle Brad has the FBI out here," Kaleb said, stifling a yawn. He drew her in one last time to kiss her before he shut the door to the truck.

"I love you," she said as he leaned away.

"I know that now, and I want you to know that I may not remember much from the past three years, but I know how much I love you," he grinned as he tapped the hood of the truck with his hand. Jessie sighed as she watched Kaleb walk to the driver's side. Her life had come full circle – finally, and she had discovered love after all: the love of a friend, the love of a brother, and the love of the man of her dreams.

Interlude 6

Her eyes flew open. It was dark. A machine was beeping. Light was filtering in from the crack under the door. The smell was familiar, sterile. An IV pole stood by her bedside. A hospital. She was in a hospital. But why? She tried to dredge up her last memory. A dark parking lot. A figure coming toward her from a bush. A sudden fear for her child's life. Her child. She had been pregnant – thirty-seven weeks along. She became alarmed and felt her stomach. She was not pregnant now. Where was her baby? Her heart began to race wildly as she panicked. The machine sounded an alarm, and the door burst open, flooding the room with light.

A nurse had come in to check the alarm, but at the sight of Dara sitting up in bed staring at her wide-eyed, the nurse passed out, falling with a great thud to the ground. Another nurse happened to be walking down the hall when she heard the sound. She entered the room cautiously, turning on the light as she entered. She chuckled, a bright smile arching across her plump black face.

"Mercy me! You're finally awake!" She stepped over the other nurse, stopping at Dara's bedside. "You must be scared right outta' your britches, child." She pushed the call button to the nurse's station.

"How can I help you?" came the hesitant voice from the intercom.

"Sara. It's Agnes. Our Sleepin' Beauty is awake, and Carol has passed out on the floor. Bring some smellin' salts and call for the doc." She patted Dara on the shoulder in an effort to smooth her wrinkled nerves.

"My baby. Where's my baby?" Agnes smiled in response.

"Oh darlin'. She's alive and well. A real beauty she is, just like her mama. I s'pose she's at home right now, sleepin' as a child should be." Dara was still confused.

"Oh honey-child. You've been in a coma for four years now. Your baby's done grown into a little girl while you've been playin' Rip Van Winkle." Dara could scarcely believe the news. Four years? She remembered nothing.

"What happened?"

"Well now, that is the mystery. S'pose you were attacked or took a bad fall. Musta hit your head somethin' fierce. A co-worker found you not twenty-minutes after she'd said g'night to you. Called 911. They took the baby c-section, but you never woke up. You were transferred here to LT after a while. Near as anyone could tell you were healthy as a horse – breathin' on your own, brain function normal. A bona fide medical mystery, you are."

The doctor arrived then, and Carol had been revived and whisked out of the room. As the doctor examined Dara, Agnes said, "S'pose I have a phone call to make."

"Wait. What time is it?"

"'Bout two o'clock in the mornin'."

"Don't call him this early, please. He'll think something terrible has happened. Just let him sleep. When does he usually come to visit? I mean, he does come to visit, right?" Agnes laughed.

"Every mornin' at 7:30 sharp. He and Hope drop by to say g'morning before he goes to work. Sometimes he drops by at lunch, and every night after dinner for a bedtime story."

"Hope?"

"He named her Hope when she was born. She brings you a daily dose of dandelion." Dara liked the name.

"Maybe I could take a shower and make myself a little more – presentable. Surprise them?"

"Sure thing, sugar. I'll be back when the doc's done."

***

7:27. . . 7:28 . . . 7:30 . . . 7:31. She was watching the clock nervously. He was late. Her heart was racing, and she was glad she was no longer hooked up to the heart monitor because the alarms would surely be sounding. She wasn't sure why she was so nervous. She had known Patrick all of her life, and they had been married for five years before the accident. They had struggled to have a family of their own, but at long last, she found out she was pregnant. She could still remember the look of joy on his face when she had told him.

But now – he had been a single father for four years. Dara realized how much could have changed in those four years. She was suddenly struck by the fact that she had no idea who the President of the United States was. What else had she missed, aside from seeing Hope's first smile, her first footsteps, her first birthday, her first tooth? They would be strangers to each other – the only link they had was Patrick. Patrick. She felt light years now separated them, and yet he had been by her side the entire time, committed, devoted, and unconditionally loving her. He hadn't given up on her, though she couldn't imagine how difficult life must have been for him. He was constant and true just as he had always been. Yet still, she was a bundle of nerves, as nervous as she had been on their first date. She glanced at the clock. 7:41. Maybe he wasn't coming. She was looking out the window when she heard little footsteps skipping down the hallway.

"Hope, honey. Slow down please." It was Patrick's voice. She heard the nurses greet the child and her husband, beaming at the surprise that awaited them, no doubt. Hope rounded the corner, stopping abruptly when she saw Dara sitting up in bed, waiting for her. Patrick peeked in warily to see what had stopped Hope in her tracks. His eyes widened as if he were seeing a ghost. His eyes filled with tears, and he shakily picked Hope up and walked toward the bed.

"Look, Hope. Mommy's awake," he said to his daughter, his voice trembling in unbelief. Hope squirmed out of his arms and jumped up on the bed. She brushed a stray hair out of Dara's face.

"Mommy, you take long naps!" she exclaimed. Dara laughed as she hugged her daughter for the first time.

"Daddy said you were really tired, but someday you'd wake up. I'm glad you waked up, Mommy." She gave her mother a wet kiss.

"I'm glad I waked up too," Dara said as she hugged her again. A nurse appeared in the doorway.

"Hope, honey. I need some help out here with an IV pole. How about it?" She winked at Patrick as Hope jumped off the bed and ran to her side. Patrick took Dara's hands in his.

"I can hardly believe my eyes. You're really awake! How do you feel?"

"Never better, now that you're here." He gathered her up in a hug.

"You don't know how much I love you, how much I've missed you," he whispered in her ear before kissing her so tenderly she nearly melted in the warmth of his arms.

"I'm so sorry you've had to go through all this alone, Patrick." He drew her lips into a kiss again to stop her from talking anymore nonsense.

"I am so happy you're alive and talking to me. I'm the luckiest man alive! I have you and Hope."

"I like her name, by the way,"

"I thought you might. That night was the darkest night of my life, but when I heard her cry – I knew there was hope – hope for me, hope for her, and most of all, hope for you. The name seemed appropriate."

"What do you say we go home? I'm ready to be discharged, and we have a lot of catching up to do – the three of us," she smiled.

"I think that's the best idea I've heard in four years," he returned her smile as he helped her to her feet.

Chapter 9: Home

HOME

HOME. The love that houses
    a person's soul.
HOME. The refuge from
    a world of indifference.
HOME. The retreat from
    the dark precipice of loneliness.
HOME. The sanctuary filled
    with happiness and peace.
HOME. The shelter from
    the storms of strife.
HOME. An asylum from
    the prejudice of the world.
HOME. A haven of understanding
    and hope.
HOME. The place where I belong -
HOME.

~ Jessie Watson

Jessie knew she had found her happily ever after at last, not in the sense that her story was ending, but because it had finally found its beginning. Jessie thought of happily ever after differently than the definition fairytales attributed to the three small words. She knew that she would still have trials and troubles ahead, but that those were the very elements that defined happily ever after. Overcoming the obstacles and oppositions, which would be interspersed with moments of love and laughter, gave birth to true happiness. Every time she saw Kaleb, she was reminded of that.

Kaleb stayed in Bradley's house until the end of the summer when he and Shane got an apartment. Kaleb enrolled in the local university as well, and they all started their freshman year of college together. Jessie continued to stay with Bradley. On her 19th birthday, at the end of summer, Bradley presented her with two gifts. The first was a scrapbook Marci put together chronicling Jessie's life. Some of the earlier pictures, Jessie had never seen before. The seemingly monochromatic pictures of her childhood contrasted the vibrancy of those that leaped from the pages when Shane's camera came onto the scene her senior year. The second gift was the announcement that Bradley and Marci were finally engaged to be married. She was so happy for him.

Her birthday would have been complete without any other surprises. She was home with her family – that was all she had ever wanted. After cake and ice cream, Kaleb drove Jessie to their place. He was standing behind her with his arms wrapped around her.

"What are you thinking about?" he whispered in her ear.

"I'm thinking that I shouldn't be so happy. I'm wondering if this is some sort of illusion, even though I know it's not. My heart is breaking for all the others out there who were like me, born into loneliness, who will never have this chance. It hardly seems fair to them that I have so much happiness and love and hope. I feel like I'm monopolizing the world's supply." He turned her around to face him and leaned down to kiss her. No matter how many times he did that, she never got used to it. Her stomach was all butterflies and roller coaster rides.

"I thought you might be feeling that way, so I have a little surprise for you." He certainly had her attention now. He continued, "My parents left me with quite a bit of money when they died, and I want to use some of it to set up a transition house for foster kids who age out of the system. It will take a while to get all the details worked out, but Bradley and Shane's dad are willing to help me with the project. Did you know sometimes emancipated foster kids are called throwaway kids? I can't get that image out of my head. You were one of them, and I owe you my life. Literally, my heart only beats because of you. I can't imagine my life without you, and I can't stand back and watch another person slip through the cracks of our society when I know I can do something about it. But I want your help." She was crying. Her emotions were overflowing, and they had nowhere else to go. She hugged Kaleb tightly, never wanting to let him go.

"You know me almost better than I know myself, Kaleb. That would be the best present anyone could ever give me or them for that matter," she said as she pulled his face close to hers so she could kiss him again.

"Would you mind if I asked you something else?" A grin spread across his face as he spoke. She shook her head. He stepped to the edge of the small hill that overlooked his property as he told her, "Jessie, my parents have owned this land for a long time. They intended to build their dream house here. The plans had been approved, the contractors had been selected, and everything is ready and waiting. I'd like to pick up where they left off. I want to build the house, but only if you'll live here with me," he paused to look at her. He walked close to her, grabbing both of her hands in his, "Will you, Jessie? Will you live here with me as my wife?" He already knew the answer to his question would be yes. They had both known for a long time that they were already one – they couldn't be separated. One without the other would simply cease to be.

"You already know I will," she told him.

***

Jessie found that life was always changing, and she made alterations to accommodate those changes as she grew and learned. Time ticked on: seconds turned into minutes, minutes to hours, hours to days, days to weeks, weeks to months, and months to years. Jessie and Kaleb were married the following summer. The house was built. They graduated from college. The transition house was organized and opened. They were blessed with children, a boy and a girl, whom they named after Kaleb's parents, Wade and Claire. Time pressed on. Their children started school and grew older. They adopted seven-year-old twins who were foster children. Bradley and Marci were married and adopted their three children from the foster care system. Shane eventually married too. Together they managed the transition house, which they called Jessie's Place. They watched as their efforts – their love – changed lives forever. They helped newly emancipated teenagers commence their lives as adults, pointing them in the right direction by giving them love, encouragement, and support.

Life wasn't perfect. They endured their trials and troubles. They had their squabbles and arguments, but they continued to live their happily ever after. Jessie was always amazed that her heart still raced when Kaleb grabbed her hand or kissed her. Sometimes, her stomach still did cartwheels when he entered the room. Jessie came to realize that home was not a physical structure: it was a place in her heart that she could take with her wherever she went. Home was wherever she was in the presence of those she loved – her very own little patchwork family that was ever growing.

As the stopwatch of her life was winding down, Jessie remembered the most important lesson Kaleb ever taught her. One by one, person by person, we can reclaim the forgotten, the lost, the lonely, or the grieving if we look beyond our own little sphere. Most people are invisible to us only because we choose not to see them. Though unintentionally, we turn our backs on those who need us most. Then, they sink into a deep oblivion, left to make sense of the world on their own. Strand by strand, we can build and strengthen the great web of humanity that binds us all together. Each strand is intricately connected to and dependent on every other strand whether we realize it or not. We can't feel hate, love, or indifference without sending vibrations throughout the entire web of life. One person's inaction can devastate entire generations, just as one person's action can preserve entire generations.

Every person can act as a watcher, keeping an eye on the worldwide web, ensuring that no strand remains broken and alone for long. Jessie knew from her personal experience the difference that one person made not only in her life, but also the lives of her children, her friends, and everyone she had helped through Jessie's Place. While her experience was certainly extraordinary, everyone could have a Kaleb-like or a Shane-like experience. She truly believed that every story could have a happily ever after, but sometimes that happily ever after needed a little nudge from someone else to get it started.

She sighed as she concluded her thought. She reached for Kaleb's hand, now wrinkled and crooked with age and arthritis. She squeezed his hand gently, and his drooping eyelids opened. His eyes were still as blue and calm as a tropical ocean on a hot summer's day. He winked at her, and she whispered, "I love you."

Postlude

Master Burdock, Gage, and Minnion stood outside Jessie's Place and watched. They often gathered there together to draw from the strengthening of the web that occurred within the walls of that building. They had watched so many enter the doors, lost and alone, only to leave with renewed hope and budding friendships. The web had never been stronger, and Master Burdock shuddered to think of what might have happened if different choices had been made at crucial moments. He quickly let the thought slip through the thin ropes of the web. They had watched Jessie's Place thrive over the years, and they had come to love all those who volunteered there.

Master Burdock had been fascinated at the way in which Kaleb's and Dara's strands naturally intertwined themselves with each other after they had gone back to the other realm, still sensing the attachment they had in the watcher's realm. It hadn't been long after Jessie's Place opened that Dara found her way there, and Jessie put her talents to use. The two families had grown to be inseparable over the years, and Master Burdock smiled his approval as he watched them gather for the fiftieth anniversary of its opening. They were all there, wrinkled with experience and wisdom, their children grown and married, their grandchildren and great-grandchildren gathered around them as they re-told the stories of their beginnings. Master Burdock made it a point to never miss an anniversary celebration of Jessie's Place as it reminded him of his purpose and renewed his faith in the web and the people who held it together.

ABOUT THE AUTHOR

Tennille Jo Mortensen grew up in rural Idaho where she developed a passion for writing as she began composing poetry and short stories at a young age. After graduating with an MBA from Idaho State University, she became a full-time mother to two daughters. While focusing on her faith and family, she draws inspiration for writing from her everyday life. She enjoys hiking, photographing waterfalls, transforming socks into unique monkeys with needle and thread, and creating memories with her husband, children, and kooky cockapoo in Portland, Oregon.

www.ingramcontent.com/pod-product-compliance
Lightning Source LLC
Chambersburg PA
CBHW070039260626
47159CB00005B/2082

* 9 7 8 1 7 3 7 0 7 2 6 0 7 *